Murder Among the Moonflowers

A Clover Haven Mystery

Kristy T Dixon

To Neeley Reed.
Thanks for letting me borrow your name.

Chapter 1

C hopped-up fake flowers and ribbons covered the table. Bits of greenery stuck to my sleeves as I worked, and now and then, I brushed them away.

I'd come in early to get a head start on some wreaths I planned to sell online. The website had been doing well and required more attention than walk-in customers now.

"Those moonflowers out front are getting huge," Jessa said as she stepped into the back room of my flower shop, *Neeley's Flower Patch*. She tossed her purse in the corner and dropped into the folding chair beside me.

I nodded. "They're pretty, aren't they? At least in the evening. I'm glad I planted them, but I wish they bloomed during the day."

Since we sold flowers, I figured we ought to have some growing around the shop. The large white blooms were five inches wide and always caught people's attention—if they happened to come by after sunset.

Jessa tossed her black braids over her shoulder and started on a new wreath. "I'm excited for book club tonight. It feels like it's been forever since the last one."

I smiled, cocking my head. "It's been two weeks."

"Exactly. That's practically a drought for us."

"Are you dressing up?" I asked.

"You better believe it. Are you?"

"I might."

Jessa pursed her lips. "It's an eighties theme. You have to dress up."

"I'm not sure I own anything that would work, and I don't have time to get anything."

"I bet Roberta has a closet full of stuff you could wear. She never gets rid of anything."

The back door swung open and Roberta burst in, her pink shirt on inside-out and one shoe untied.

"Tell me you've heard the news about Forrest Cutler!"

I tried to remember the latest gossip I'd heard but came up empty. "Nope."

"He's trying to open a winery right here in Clover Haven."

"A winery?" Jessa said. "Oh no. That boy better think again. We don't need any of that in our town."

I pushed my long, dark brown hair over my shoulder. "Forrest always has some kind of plan. They usually fizzle out, or he loses interest halfway through."

"There's going to be a town meeting about it next week."

"I'll be there," Jessa said, threading a rose into her wreath.

I'd probably go too—if only to hear what everyone was saying. In a town this small, city council meetings were a major source of entertainment.

"Someone needs to tell the sheriff to come," Roberta added. "Last meeting, Billie punched Mr. Valenzuela in the shoulder, and it wasn't soft."

I hid a smile. I kind of wish I'd seen that.

"Is the sheriff coming to book club?" Roberta asked me.

"How would I know?"

"You two seemed friendly the last time he was here."

"I haven't talked to him in over two weeks."

Jessa cut a piece of ribbon. "Does he even know it's book club tonight?"

"Probably not." I was trying to sound neutral, but it bugged me a little that Sheriff Troy McGregor hadn't contacted me in so long. Not that I'd reached out either. Stubbornness was a team sport.

"It's weird to think the two of you were childhood friends," Roberta said. "You had us all convinced you hated him." She shook her head disapprovingly.

I grabbed more daisies. "I did. For a while."

"How does that even work?"

"I don't want to talk about it. We were best friends from kindergarten to twenty. We had a misunderstanding and didn't talk for fifteen years."

"But now you've resolved it?"

"Yes. We decided we could be friends again."

"But you haven't talked in two weeks?"

I let out a soft laugh. "You two know me. I'm not exactly a people person. I don't go out of my way to do much outside the shop and book club."

Roberta's eyes lit up. "Speaking of book club, it's going to be awesome tonight!" She attempted a Michael Jackson moonwalk and almost tripped over a bucket of fake carnations. "The eighties were my happy time."

Jessa nodded toward me. "Neeley doesn't have anything to wear."

"What? You know I've got half a closet full of my old clothes from back then. You can come over after work and pick something out. I was about half a person smaller back then, so nothing fits me now, but I keep them just in case I ever get the urge to starve myself."

"I got some little leg warmers online for Murphy," I said. "I figured if he dressed up, it counted for me too."

Jessa smiled. "That'll be so cute. Where is Murphy?"

"With my grandpa. He didn't want me to get a dog, but now he tucks Murphy in at night and watches TV with him."

"Are you going to text the sheriff?" Jessa asked.

I sighed. "I suppose... but he's probably busy solving crimes and polishing that badge."

"Try," she urged.

I pulled out my phone and sent a quick text, telling him Jessa really wanted him to come to book club. That way, if he ignored it, it wasn't my ego on the line.

"And you're going to wear something eighties?"

"If you insist."

꧁꧂

I stood in front of my mirror and grimaced. I really hoped Troy didn't come tonight. Roberta had talked me into wearing some of her old clothes, and I looked hideous. The denim jacket and jeans weren't bad, but Jessa had arranged my hair into a big, puffy mess. The bright blue eyeshadow wasn't helping either.

Roberta's clothes probably hadn't even been stylish in the actual eighties, and she hadn't made a fashionable clothing choice in all the years I'd known her. It was a win if she came into work with her shoes on the right feet.

Jessa loved fashion, but her style wasn't something I could pull off either. She'd crimped my hair and teased my bangs until they stood almost straight up.

"I wouldn't have survived the eighties," I told her, touching my stiff bangs.

"Don't touch them," she said. "You don't want to ruin the effect."

"I feel ridiculous."

"You look great. I was a teen in the eighties, and I wore the eighties well. The nineties, not so much, but I had the eighties down."

"I've never had any of it right," Roberta admitted. "As soon as I catch on to a fashion trend, it's already over."

"Murphy looks awesome," Jessa said, scooping him up and cuddling him. He had on tiny leg warmers and a sweatband across his forehead. He might have been the cutest pug of all time—and the most patient.

"Should we go? People are probably already here."

We held book club in one of the unused rooms in my grandpa's mortuary. It was a dark space with a long table, lit by candles to make it feel cozier. Not too cozy, though. We were reading mysteries after all. Every week, we read a different one and usually discussed half the book on Tuesday and the other half on Friday.

"Is Sheriff McGregor coming?" Jessa asked as we walked down the hallway.

"He never responded. He's probably on duty."

Jessa wore an oversized New Kids on the Block T-shirt, her hair even bigger than mine, and her makeup edging into Cleopatra territory. Roberta had tied a knot on the side of her shirt and was rocking the same blue eyeshadow I was. Her brown side ponytail bounced on her shoulder.

We stepped into the book club room. That was what we all called it, anyway. The mortuary was huge, and the third floor was where Grandpa and I lived. The book club room hadn't been used for anything until I claimed it.

Jim, Patty, and Lydia were already in their seats, all dressed up except for Jim, who looked like he'd wandered in from the nineties by mistake. We chatted in small groups until Billie arrived. Geneva had dropped out, so we were down to seven members—eight if you counted Troy, but since he'd only come twice, that was debatable.

At thirty-five, I was the youngest member of the group. Lydia was around forty, and the others were in their fifties and sixties. Honestly, I preferred them to hanging out with most people my age.

"The muffins smell good," Patty said.

Lydia beamed. "I hope they are. I spent all afternoon on them, so please eat a lot. Preferably in bulk."

"Okay," I said. "Today we're talking about *A Totally Killer Wedding* by D.A. Wilkerson."

"Beckett is my kind of hero," Roberta said. "She can fall on her face and still make progress. I love reading about someone as clumsy as I am."

"You do seem to have a lot of accidents," Patty said. "More than the average person."

"My parents always told me I'd grow into my awkward limbs, but unfortunately, they were wrong."

Murphy started running around the room with his tongue hanging out. He was hard to ignore when he got like this—snorting, crashing into the walls, and having the time of his life.

"Calm down, Murph," I said, holding out my arms. He ignored me and kept circling. "Sorry. He does this about once a day."

Lydia smiled. "He's so cute. If I ever get a dog—which I won't—it'll be a pug."

"They stink," Billie said. "All dogs do."

We all did our best to ignore Billie.

"I love a book about a murder at a wedding," Patty said.

Jessa frowned. "Really? That seems so sad."

Patty shrugged. "But fun when it's a book."

"No one spoil anything if you finished it!" Roberta said. "I'm only halfway."

I always finished the book in one day, so I had to be careful when we got to discussing. I didn't understand how anyone could read a book slowly.

"I finished it," Jim said. "I'll keep it to myself. Have you finished, Billie?"

Billie fluffed her short gray curls. "Not this time. I'm about two-thirds there."

Jim's eyes lit up. "You always say you guess the murderer right from the start. Why don't you write down who you think did it, and we'll hide the paper and check it at the next meeting?"

Billie glared. "That's ridiculous."

Jim chuckled, slapping his hands on his thighs. "That's what I thought."

"Who was everyone's favorite side character?" I asked, trying to take the pressure off her.

"Starla, hands down," Jessa said.

"Oh yeah!" Patty held out her hand, and they high-fived. "Starla's fun."

"I liked Greg," Jim said.

Lydia frowned. "There wasn't anyone named Greg."

Jim rolled his eyes. "Come on! I thought he'd be the one everyone was talking about. He might be a potential love interest down the road."

"I don't remember him," Lydia said.

"The youth pastor?" I said, trying to help.

"Ohhh! I thought his name was Gary. I need to get my eye prescription checked. I just turned forty, and I swear everything on me has fallen apart this year."

"Oh, to be forty again," Patty said. "I could still move back then."

"You think he might be a love interest?" Lydia asked. "Since when do you care about love interests, Jim?"

Jim laughed. "I don't. I just know the lot of you care an awful lot about stuff like that."

"Beckett deserves love," Roberta said with a sigh, "but don't we all?"

Jessa patted Roberta's arm, and Roberta gave her a small, sad smile. Roberta and I were the only two in the group who had never been married. Most of the others had lost their spouses—or, in Billie's case, divorced. Lydia was the only one who was currently married.

"I hope there's some love for her," Patty said. "I guess we'll have to keep reading to see."

"I like Frank," Billie said.

I wrinkled my nose. "The slightly unqualified policeman?"

"Yep. Something about him is fun." She paused, visibly thinking for a moment. "Could he be a love interest?"

Jim waved a dismissive hand and snorted. "No way. How old was he supposed to be?"

"I don't know. Does age matter when love is involved?"

"It's not going to happen."

I didn't offer an opinion. Since I'd already finished the book, I might have had more insight than the others, and I didn't want to spoil anything.

Murphy barked and started running around the room again.

"I don't think Murphy likes dress-up," Jim said. "You should take his leg warmers off."

Patty scooped him up. "I think he likes them. He's just eager to find out who the killer is."

Jessa laughed. "I doubt Neeley reads the books out loud to him."

A smile tugged at my lips. I didn't—but it might not be a bad idea.

Chapter 2

I gave Forrest Cutler a tight smile as he stood across the counter in my flower shop, going on about his dream of opening a winery in Clover Haven. I wasn't sure why he'd stopped by, but he'd been talking for a while. I'd zoned out five minutes ago, and he hadn't noticed.

"That's why I think it would be a great addition to the town," he finished. "Do I have your support?"

My guess was that he was going around trying to get people on his side before the town meeting.

"Umm, I'll have to think about it."

"You know we'd need fresh flowers—and this is where we'd get them."

I'd never been to a winery, but I couldn't picture one needing flowers.

"We'll have some of the best wines in the country. It might put Clover Haven on the map. What's your favorite wine?"

"I don't drink."

"Everyone drinks."

I shrugged. "I don't."

Forrest sighed. "Well, I hope you'll come out and be supportive of an old friend."

He held out his hand, and I shook it. He kept hold of it longer than necessary, rubbing his thumb over my knuckles. I cringed and pulled away.

Jessa came in from the back. "You think we need more drunks running around town?"

Forrest straightened his collar. "Most people drink responsibly."

"I'm against it. We have a nice little town here, and you might ruin that. It'll bring people in, and that's something we don't need."

"Growth is inevitable. You might as well embrace it, not fear it."

Jessa took a breath, and I braced myself for a lecture.

Forrest must have seen it coming too, because he cut her off. "What do you suppose Sheriff McGregor will think?"

I shrugged. "You'll have to ask him."

"You two were tight in school. I figure you know what he thinks about these things."

"We haven't had a lot of contact in the last fifteen years."

"Does he drink wine?"

"Not that I know of." People might think it was lame, but Troy, our best friend Chase, and I had made a promise back in seventh grade that we'd stay away from alcohol. I couldn't say if they'd stuck to it—but I had.

"You should leave. Or buy some flowers," Jessa said.

"Alright. I hope I have your support." He left the store, and the door slammed shut behind him.

"He's delusional if he thinks I support him," Jessa said, tossing her braids over her shoulder.

I rubbed my hand against my jeans. "I went to school with him. He was always that way."

"You didn't date him or anything, right?"

I gave a dry laugh. "I went to a dance with him once."

"On purpose?"

"He asked me, and I didn't want to be rude." I didn't add that I also didn't want to be the only person I knew who hadn't ever gone to a dance. Troy and Chase had been asked to every single one, whether it was girl's choice or not. That was what happened when your graduating class had way more girls than boys. Because I'd mostly spent time with just the two of them, any flirting on my part had been lighthearted—and always directed at them.

"Did you ever go to a dance with the sheriff?"

I tried to smile. "No. We were just friends." I'd wanted to go to every dance with him.

"It's about time to close," Jessa said. "I'll walk up to the mortuary with you."

Jessa worked a few hours at my shop and a few at the mortuary.

By the time I left her at the front desk, I had just enough time to go over some paperwork. I'd worked part-time for my grandpa since I was fifteen, doing whatever needed to be done—which usually meant paperwork.

I went upstairs, got Murphy from Grandpa, and headed to my room. Since I lived and worked here, I did most things in my room, from the comfort of my bed. I had a small desk, but I preferred my mattress.

Getting comfortable, I climbed onto my bed and pulled out my laptop. I stared at all the files Grandpa had sent me, but I couldn't help wondering why Troy hadn't even texted to say he couldn't come. Not that it mattered.

Murphy came to the bed and whimpered.

"Look, pal. I love you, but you are a little gross. Every time you get on my bed, I feel like I need to wash everything."

He whined, and I reached down to pick him up. I needed a decoy blanket—something I could toss off the bed when Murphy wasn't around. He scooted in at my side and curled up.

"You know you're needy?" I patted his head. "I guess that's okay. I might need to do this later. My mind isn't into it."

My phone rang, and I sighed when I saw Jim's name. He never called unless he wanted to get me to do something I didn't want to do.

"Hi, Jim."

"Hello, Neeley. I have a favor to ask."

"Oh?" I pushed the laptop away.

"There's going to be a big town meeting to talk about Forrest and his winery. We think it's going to be heavily attended. Do you think you could fill the dessert tables?"

"Sure," I said, relieved. Jim had asked me to do some annoying things over the years, but this was something I could manage.

"Thanks. I knew I could count on you. Talk to you later."

"Bye."

I put the phone down and realized I'd missed a text from Troy.

"What's your excuse?" I muttered. I read it aloud to Murphy. "Sorry to miss book club. Maybe next time." I stared at the screen for a moment, then turned the phone off. "He didn't even give an excuse."

Murphy tilted his head and looked up at me.

"Yes, I know. I have issues. Let's change subjects, alright? What should we make for the town meeting? It has to be something I can make a lot of and won't take too long... That means cookies. Lots and lots of cookies."

Murphy snorted and licked his nose. That seemed to be one of his talents.

"Did I lock the flower shop?" I asked. "Dang it." I had a thing about locks. I checked them several times before I was satisfied, and then I still worried about whether I'd done it. If it crossed my mind after I got home, I had to go back and check. In all the times I'd done it, the door had never been unlocked—yet I still had to go.

"Come on, Murph. We're going to have to check so I can sleep tonight."

He jumped off the bed, and I grabbed his leash. We made it to the shop in good time, and I was surprised to see Vivian Cutler—Forrest's wife—standing out front, admiring my moonflowers. It was strange to see anyone here after hours. We were a mile from the heart of town, and there wasn't much reason to be out this way unless someone needed flowers or a funeral.

Vivian gave me a tight smile. "Lovely flowers."

"Thanks."

"Moonflowers?"

"Yes."

"I've always loved them." She sounded almost wistful.

I nodded, waiting for her to tell me why she was here.

She fiddled with her hands for a moment before asking, "Has Forrest come to talk to you, by chance?"

"He was here earlier."

"Can I ask you something?"

"Sure."

"I'm not native to this area, and I don't know a lot of people. Most folks know you, right?"

"Most. At least by name, because of the shop and the mortuary."

"I was wondering if you could convince people the winery is a bad idea."

I frowned. "You don't want Forrest to go through with it?"

"No. He's had a lot of dumb ideas over the years, and most of them lose us money. This one's going to take everything we have, and if it fails, we lose everything."

"Have you tried talking to him?"

Vivian nodded and unconsciously began braiding her brown hair. "I've talked myself hoarse. He's so sure it'll work, he won't listen. I even made him talk to a financial advisor, and they told him it was a bad idea. He got angry and refused to go back."

"I'm not sure I can influence anyone. Most folks already have strong opinions one way or the other."

"I'd talk to people myself, but this town sticks with its locals. I've never been able to break into the little cliques around here."

"Is it that bad? I'm from here, so I guess I wouldn't notice."

"It's bad."

"I'm sorry. That must be hard. You're welcome to join my book club if you want. It's full of opinionated people, but they're fun and nice."

"I'll think about it. I'm not much of a reader."

"You're welcome anytime."

Murphy tried to pull away, so I pushed on the front door of the shop. Locked, as usual.

"Do you know anyone who might help me?" she asked.

"Hmm. Jackie Pearson owns the diner. If a winery comes to town, it might pull business away from her. She's loud and good at being in people's business."

"What about the mayor? Do you know his opinion on this?"

"No idea. I know he drinks wine occasionally."

"So maybe not my ally." Her mouth turned down. "What about the sheriff?"

"I think he might be on your side."

"Forrest said Sheriff McGregor was good friends with you."

"Yeah. When we were younger. Back then, he was against drinking altogether. It's been years since I've heard his thoughts on it, so I can't say for sure. Jessa works with me—she's been going around telling everyone to vote against it. You might want to talk to her."

She nodded. "Is the reason you don't want to interfere because you support the winery? Forrest told me the two of you dated in high school. Maybe you share his vision?"

I made a face. "We didn't date. We went to one dance."

Her eyes narrowed. "I know he had a huge crush on you."

I wrinkled my nose. "I didn't know that. We hardly ever talked. Like I said, one dance."

"You didn't have anything for him? No crush?"

"Not in a million years." I realized how rude that sounded and tried to backpedal. "Nothing against Forrest. I was just interested in someone else at the time."

She glanced back at the flowers. "I get that. Well, I won't bother you anymore."

I watched her drive off in a car that probably cost more than my flower shop. That might've been an exaggeration—but not by much.

"Come on, Murph. Let's try to get some work done." I rarely struggled to stay focused, so I blamed the weather.

We plodded up the hill to the mortuary. No one could miss it—a large black building with two turrets, like something out of a vampire movie. I'd lived there my whole life and still had to take in the place every time I approached it. When I was a kid, I used to bring friends over and we would tell ghost stories just to scare ourselves.

"You coming, Murphy?"

He'd found a caterpillar and was sniffing at it with interest.

I tried not to think about the fact that Forrest had liked me back in high school. I shouldn't have been surprised.

He'd tried to talk to me and sat by me in a few classes, but I'd always assumed my standoffish vibe had done the trick.

"We've got things to do. You coming?"

He gave the caterpillar one last sniff and finally trotted over at my coaxing.

Chapter 3

The room at the town hall felt like it would burst at the seams. I was almost sure there were more people inside than legally allowed, but Troy wasn't kicking anyone out. I hadn't talked to him, but I'd seen him walking the perimeter.

Mayor Branson stood at the front of the room, watching people chat in small groups. Chairs had been stuffed in as tightly as they could go. Refreshments were in the next room over, and if I said so myself, they looked pretty great. Since the meeting hadn't started yet, I went back in to make sure everything was perfect.

The room was large and plain, which made it useful for a lot of things. We'd even had town dances here a few times. I'd set up three tables—two were covered with cookies and brownies. Roberta and Jessa had found out about my assignment and helped me bake them.

Two large punch bowls of cider sat on the third table; a bouquet of moonflowers I'd arranged decorated the center. I hoped they'd stay open, but it was anyone's guess.

Jackie Pearson, the diner owner, had volunteered to help pour cider into cups. She was already setting some out on the table.

"It looks nice," she said. "The flowers are so pretty."

"Thanks. And thanks for offering to help."

"Sure thing. I was going to be here anyway—I might as well make myself useful."

"You're coming in for the meeting, right?"

She set down the ladle and rearranged the cups. "You better believe it. I always make sure I know what's going on in town."

"Are you going to speak?" I figured she had the most to lose.

"Nah. I don't really care one way or another. I mean, I don't sell much alcohol at the diner."

We entered the meeting room and found seats in the back. The mayor was calling everyone to order as we sat. He explained the purpose of the meeting and that questions would be welcome at the end, then let Forrest tell everyone why he believed a winery would benefit Clover Haven.

I tried to listen, but I kept watching Troy to see what he thought. He had never been a fan of Forrest, and he was frowning as he listened. I wondered what he'd do if I went over and pushed his sandy blond hair back. I shook my head and told myself to stop daydreaming.

After Forrest finished, the mayor opened the floor for comments. Each person had one minute.

Pedro Valenzuela, the small grocery store owner, stood first. "We don't have the population to support a winery. It'll just go out of business. Besides, there are people like me and Jackie whose businesses will be hurt if it comes in." He sat back down.

Damion Burton stood next. "Forrest is irresponsible and burns through family money fast. Has anything he's tried ever worked? No. He's going to build a gigantic building, lose everything, and the town will be stuck with an eyesore."

Patty stood and twisted her handkerchief. "It'll ruin the nice, cozy feel of the town. I've researched it—it would bring in more people, and we don't like that here. We don't need any more drunks, either."

Forrest's mouth tightened, and he crossed his arms. The mayor reminded him he couldn't interrupt, and Forrest looked like he might explode.

Bruce Hudson stood up. "There's nothing wrong with a winery. You all don't want change, but change happens. We voted down that new store, and it went to the next town instead. Now they get all the benefits. This winery could be great for us."

Forrest grinned.

"And you'll be drunk in the gutter more often!" someone shouted from the crowd.

More people spoke. Most were opposed, but a few were for it. I figured a lot of folks were like me—mildly against it, but not enough to get worked up. I just didn't think it would succeed here.

Vivian slipped in and sat across from us in the back row. She rubbed her eyes and yawned, nodding along with everyone who opposed the plan. I couldn't help feeling bad for her. Honestly, I'd feel bad for anyone married to Forrest.

After everyone had their say, the mayor called for a silent vote. He always did these, and they were completely pointless. He counted them up, then he and the city council did whatever they wanted anyway. The majority seemed to be against Forrest's idea.

I hurried to the next room and stood behind the refreshment table. People started filing in, chatting. I hoped we'd made enough and cringed when someone grabbed five cookies. We were probably fine—but still. It stressed me.

Vivian and Forrest walked in arm in arm, but neither looked particularly happy. I wondered if they'd had a fight. They headed for the cider and started talking to Bruce

Hudson. Vivian smiled, but it looked forced, not quite meeting her eyes.

"Cookies!" Troy said, grabbing one and shoving the whole thing into his mouth. Some things never changed.

I smiled. "Most people bite them and try to enjoy it."

"I guess. I've never been most people."

"What did you think?" I asked.

"About the cookie or the meeting?" He came around to my side of the table so he wouldn't block anyone.

"Both."

"Well, as usual, your cookies are perfect. As for the meeting... I don't know. I'm against the winery. The mayor already knows my opinion. It just feels like something that'll give me more work. Not that everyone who drinks wine is a drunk, but giving people like Bruce more options doesn't sit right with me."

"This cider is bad," I heard someone say. I looked over to see Vivian peering into her cup with disgust. "Don't drink it, Forrest."

"It tastes fine," he said, draining his cup.

"No one drink the cider!" Vivian called out. "I think it's bad."

I tilted my head. "I tasted it. It's fine."

Vivian shook her head. "No, it's definitely bad." She handed her cup to Forrest. "Dump that."

Forrest drained her cup, too. "You're imagining things, Viv."

Vivian grabbed the large punch bowl and tried to walk with it. It was awkwardly big and full, and her heels weren't up for it. Cider sloshed all over her, and then she dropped the whole thing as her wet hands struggled to grip it.

I cringed at the sound of my expensive glass bowl shattering.

"Great," she muttered, shaking cider off her arms. She turned to Forrest. "I'm going to clean myself up."

"No one move!" Jessa called out. "Stay away from the glass." She bent to pick up the larger pieces while Troy grabbed a garbage can from the corner and helped her.

"Sorry, everyone," Forrest said. "Vivian's high-strung."

I wanted to tell him he owed me a hundred dollars, but that could wait. Someone brought over a mop and waited while the glass was cleared.

I pulled the cookie tables farther back so people could still get treats without walking through the mess. Cleanup went quickly, and conversation picked back up like nothing had happened. In Clover Haven, a town meeting didn't end when it was over—it turned into a social event. Forty-five minutes later, the room still buzzed with activity.

Forrest laughed at someone's joke, loud enough to drown out everyone else.

"That wasn't even a funny joke," Jessa muttered beside me.

"I didn't hear it."

"You're lucky."

"Can someone get me a drink?" Forrest called out. "My mouth is disgustingly dry."

Someone handed him a cup. It was a good thing I'd made two bowls of cider.

Troy came up behind us. "I'll have Forrest pay for the bowl."

I shrugged. "It's annoying, but not a huge deal."

"Rats!" Forrest shouted. He jumped onto the drink table, spilling cups. "Do something about the rats!"

"Lovely," Jessa said, rolling her eyes. "More to clean up."

"There aren't any rats," someone called.

"This is why we don't need more access to alcohol," Patty added. "I bet he spiked his drink."

"Something's going on," Troy said, scanning the room. "Where's Vivian?"

Jessa pointed at the door. "She was soaked. She went home to change."

"Forrest, get off the table," Troy said, stepping in front of him. "There are no rats."

Forrest's eyes darted around the room. "I saw them. Everywhere."

"Get down."

He jumped down and scowled.

"Now clean this up."

"That's not my job." He snorted, arrogance lacing his words.

Troy put his hands on his hips. "You made the mess."

Forrest blinked a few times. "I think I need a doctor. I feel funny." Sweat rolled down his forehead, and a sickly pallor clung to his skin. He stumbled carelessly across the floor.

"I'll take you," Troy offered.

"I don't need help from Troy McGregor," he said, looking around wildly. "You're the reason Neeley couldn't see me."

Troy placed a hand on his arm. "Forrest? We need to get you out of here."

Forrest's eyes went wide. He shook his head. "The sheriff has horns! And look at all the rats!" He bolted across the room and ran out the front door.

Troy hurried after him.

"What was that all about?" Jessa asked.

I shrugged. "With Forrest? Who knows?"

A high-pitched scream outside brought the room to a halt.

Jessa and I exchanged a look.

"What do you suppose—" I took a step toward the door and paused.

Troy ran back in. "I want everyone to stay here until I say so." He disappeared again.

I rubbed my arm, goosebumps rising.

Everyone stood still, murmuring quietly.

Vivian came tearing into the room, tears streaming down her face, with lines of makeup running down her cheeks.

"What's wrong, Mrs. Cutler?" Patty asked, stepping forward.

"Forrest just got hit by a car! He's dead."

A hush fell over the room.

Patty gasped and rushed to comfort her.

I took a shaky breath and looked around. What had just happened? Forrest had been acting so strange—it was almost like he'd been drunk.

We waited for what felt like forever until we finally heard sirens. Thirty minutes later, Troy came back in and said we could leave.

He paced the room while people filed out slowly. An officer entered and escorted Vivian away soon after.

Jessa gathered the platters and tablecloths while I promised to finish the rest.

Soon, the only people left were me and Troy—and he was still pacing. He must've seen the whole thing.

I walked over and stood in front of him so he'd have to stop. "Are you all right?"

He nodded, but I wasn't convinced.

I tilted my head. "For real?"

"I shouldn't have chased him out. He might—" He rubbed a hand over his eyes.

"Don't, Troy. It wasn't your fault."

"But—"

"No. He would've run whether you chased him or not. Something weird was going on." I wanted to sound reassuring, but I was shaken too. If we were friends again, I figured that meant I could hug him. I used to do it all the time, so I wrapped my arms around him, and he clung to me.

I gave him a squeeze. "Don't they teach you in the academy that these things happen?"

"Yeah, but, man. That was so... I'm going to have nightmares."

"I'm sorry. But it wasn't your fault." I rubbed his back, and memories came rushing in. We'd always been there for each other, and I was annoyed at myself for ruining that for so many years.

Then I felt him nod into my hair.

He released me and took a deep breath. "I'm all right. Let me help you with your bowl."

We walked to the table, and I frowned as I glanced into the remaining cider bowl. A moonflower floated on the surface. A chill ran through my entire body.

"What is it?" he asked.

I reached in and pulled out the wet bloom. "These are toxic."

"It wasn't in there earlier."

"No. But what if one was in the other bowl and I didn't notice? It would take a lot to kill someone, but it could cause hallucinations... like maybe someone thinking they saw rats."

Troy shook his head. "It must've fallen in at the end. We would've seen one on the ground if it had been in the other bowl."

A tight knot formed in my stomach, and I pressed my hand against it. "Vivian said the cider tasted bad. They were the first ones to drink it, so no one else got any. You should have her taken to the hospital—just to be safe."

"Wouldn't she have already shown symptoms?"

"Probably. But should we risk it?" I rubbed the ache at my stomach. It only seemed to grow more violent.

Troy's frown deepened. "Probably not. I'll take care of it." He picked up the bowl and carried it to my car as I trailed him. "I'll come check on you after I deal with Vivian."

I nodded and climbed inside. This was all my fault. Why had I decorated with moonflowers? I'd done it so many times over the years and it had never been a problem. I shook my head. There had to be another explanation. Troy was probably right. There hadn't been flowers in the bowl. At least, not that I'd seen.

Still... something had happened to Forrest. And I wanted to know what.

Chapter 4

"You're not dressed up," Patty said to me at book club a few days later.

"No," I said, "but Murphy is."

Murphy ran over to her and begged for her lap. Patty was quickly becoming one of his favorites. She picked him up and laughed when he licked her face.

Vivian was fine, but she didn't want Forrest's body tested since a car had hit him. Troy was trying to convince her it might be important, but she thought it was a waste of time. He'd appealed to a judge, but that could take a while. He was convinced Forrest had been on something, and if that turned out to be true, it could change how things were handled.

"I love your earrings," I told Patty.

She smiled and rubbed the large hoops. "My favorite thing about the eighties."

Jim and Roberta came in, and Roberta placed a plate of banana bread on the table. The others filed in behind them, and I flipped on the hot chocolate maker. I rarely used it, so I decided to leave it in here for now.

"Has everyone finished the book now?" I asked.

Heads bobbed around the room.

"Great. Consensus?"

"I loved it," Lydia said. "I have hopes for romance in the next book or two."

Jim grinned. "Ah, but with whom?"

"Beckett and... I'm not sure yet. I have a feeling, but I've been surprised before."

"There might not be a big romance," Jim said. "It's not required."

"But I have hope," Patty added.

Troy slipped in. He must've been off duty—he wore jeans and a blue T-shirt. "Sorry I'm late."

"We're discussing the possible romance in the book," I told him.

Troy cringed. "I hate reading romance."

"Oh, is the poor sheriff bitter?" Lydia teased.

"I'm not bitter."

"Not enough love in your life?"

Troy smiled. "I've just never enjoyed reading romance."

"But have you ever had any?"

He chuckled. "Any romance? Aren't we supposed to be talking about a book?"

"Oh, dear!" Lydia pressed a dramatic hand to her heart. "The poor sheriff has never been in love!"

"Don't tease the boy," Billie said. "Not everyone gets to fall in love."

Troy rolled his eyes. "I've been in love."

I raised my eyebrows. I wasn't surprised—I just didn't know about it. Fifteen years of Troy's life were a mystery to me. Still, I hoped he wouldn't talk about it. It wasn't something I wanted to hear.

"How many times?" Roberta asked. "I've been in love at least ten times, but it never went in my favor."

Troy shrugged. "Once."

Jessa shook her head and protested, "There's no way someone as gorgeous as you has only been in love once."

We all laughed, Troy included. It had always been hard to embarrass him.

He winked. "Thanks, Jessa. You boost my self-esteem."

"So, tell us about it," Patty said.

Troy crossed his arms and leaned back in his chair. "I don't think that's why we're here."

"But if we all want to know about it, that's what matters."

I didn't want to hear about it, but if I said anything, I'd look like the jealous, crazy friend.

"It started a long time ago," he said. "There's really nothing to it. I fell in love with her, she didn't feel the same."

"I don't believe it," Jessa said. "Any woman would take you. If I were fifteen years younger..."

He chuckled. "I never told her. She never showed any sign of feeling the same."

Relief flooded me, and I knew that made me a terrible friend.

"Lame," Lydia said. "You should've said something and given her a chance to decide."

"Agreed," Jim said. "I never thought the sheriff was a wimp."

Troy gave a side grin. "I'm not a wimp. It was a long time ago."

"Is she married?" Patty asked. "Could you try now?"

He chuckled. "She's not married. But it was a lifetime ago."

"Tell us her name, we'll fix it," Jessa pushed.

His grin widened. "Never."

"So you don't think about her anymore?" Lydia asked.

"No more than once or twice a day. Maybe more on the days I see her."

Billie clicked her tongue. "Not acceptable. A man like you needs love."

"A man like me? What's that supposed to mean?"

"It means we'll find the girl and make things happen."

I shook my head. "Leave him alone. Let's get back to the book." I didn't want to think about Troy pining away after someone. It made my stomach twist. And if he still saw her, that meant she was around.

"Maybe he needs someone new," Roberta said. "My niece is coming to town soon. She's your age."

He groaned. "No. I don't do setups."

"Why not?"

"I don't want to."

"That's because you're being a wimp."

"You all need to quit calling me a wimp. I just don't like to date. I'm busy, and why should I date someone if I'm going to be wishing they were someone else?"

Billie shook her head. "We must find out who that woman is and fix the sheriff."

He snorted. "I don't need to be fixed."

"You sound just as sad as Neeley," Jessa said. "She's got the same 'Oh poor me, I can only fall in love once and now I'll die alone' energy."

I tilted my head. "Ha ha. I'm not like that."

"That's true," Roberta said. "She's more of the 'I lost my chance at love and now I don't need a man—watch me unclog the toilet and overhaul the radiator' variety."

I rolled my eyes and smiled. "You two are ridiculous."

"So why aren't we trying to pry out who Neeley was in love with?" Troy asked.

I smiled. "Everyone knows I'm not going there."

"I'd like to hear," Jim said.

There was no way I was going to tell them I'd been crazy in love with Troy when I was younger. And I definitely wasn't going to tell them that as soon as he came back into my life, all those feelings came rushing back. So, I shook my head. "I'd like to go back to talking about Beckett."

For the rest of book club, I was distracted, wondering who Troy had been in love with. It was probably better I didn't know. Knowing would just irritate me. I hoped it wasn't anyone I'd gone to school with.

Troy was the last to leave. He sat on the floor and played with Murphy.

"Do you want more hot chocolate?" I asked. "There's about a cup left."

"Sure," he said, standing.

I handed him a cup. "I think we should get mugs. Matching book club mugs. Then we won't be using Styrofoam all the time."

"But you'll have to wash them."

"True. But it might be worth it."

He took a sip. "Are you gonna tell me who you were in love with?"

I scoffed. "Never."

"Is it someone I knew?"

I rubbed my lips together.

"That means yes. Please tell me it wasn't Forrest."

I wrinkled my nose and shoved his shoulder for even suggesting such a thing. "No way."

"He liked you in high school."

"So I hear."

"Why won't you tell me?"

"I've never told anyone. Why would I tell you?" I'd lied without meaning to. I'd forgotten I told Grandpa.

"Because I'm your best friend."

"You didn't tell me who you were in love with."

"Yeah, but that's because it's complicated."

"McKenzie Taylor, huh?" I laughed at the look on his face. McKenzie drove him crazy—and not in a good way.

"Not in a hundred years." He wrinkled his nose and mock-shivered. "Let's go back to you. Tell me it wasn't Chase..."

A smile tugged at my lips. "It wasn't Chase."

"That's a relief. I mean, Chase is one of my best friends, but that would've been weird."

"Did you find anything out about Forrest?" I asked, changing the subject.

Troy's smile fell. "No. We need to see if he had any drugs or anything in his system."

"I'm nervous about that. What if it was something from the moonflowers?"

"Even if it was, you didn't put them in the cider." He took a sip of the hot chocolate.

"But I brought them. Everyone always compliments them, so I always use them for decorations. I'm not going to anymore. I might even dig them up."

"Is that what's growing outside your shop?"

"Yes."

"I don't think the flowers are to blame. I think he must've been on drugs."

"I'm going to be stressed until we find out."

"I'm hoping we'll get permission to do the toxicology. Then we should know more."

"I wonder why Vivian's against it."

"She told me she doesn't want to find out he was into drugs or something like that. She's worried about how it'll look to everyone else in town."

I shifted. "I know she struggles with fitting in around here. I never thought much about it, but I guess we are a tight little community. It must be hard for people who move in—we're kind of set in our ways."

"It's doubtful she'll stay. She said she will, but I'd be surprised. All her family is back East. She used to have a good job there, and she said they'd take her back. Right now, I think she's in shock and not sure what to do."

"They have a nice house."

"And it's paid for, so she might stay. But I still think she'll sell. From what she told me, she hates it here."

"Why did she come?"

"She met Forrest at a convention in her hometown. They lived here because he already owned the house. She said she was a little worried he might've been dabbling in something—he's been acting funny and—"

"Isn't book club over?" Grandpa asked, ambling into the room.

"Since when do you care about book club?" I asked.

He smiled. "Since me and Murphy started watching reruns in the evenings." Murphy ran over, and Grandpa scooped him up.

"Hello, Walt," Troy said.

Grandpa scowled. "Remember how you almost never came around for over a decade?" He let the words sink in for an uncomfortable moment. "I miss those days."

He was never going to like Troy.

"Grandpa, don't be rude."

"I wasn't being rude, just making an observation."

Troy grinned as Grandpa left the room. "He never changes."

"Sorry."

"I always thought it was funny."

"Yeah, you and Chase were strange that way. I avoid people who don't like me, you seem to seek them out for your own amusement."

"I get why he doesn't like me. I was an obnoxious kid. You weren't any better, though, and he likes you."

"He has to like me. You have to make exceptions for family. Besides, I was well behaved when you and Chase weren't with me. So maybe you brought it out in me."

"Or you brought it out in us."

"I haven't caused trouble in years!" I protested.

He grinned. "I don't believe that. If it's true, the real you must be bursting to escape. Wanna go toilet paper something?"

"Wouldn't you have to arrest yourself?"

He winked. "Probably."

Chapter 5

"Good morning!" Jackie Pearson said, floating into my shop. Her blond hair fell over her shoulder in a French braid, and she looked happier than I'd seen her in a while. Not that she was usually unhappy, but she often gave off a bored vibe.

I smiled. "Hello. How are things today?"

"Wonderful. I've had so much stress lately, and a lot of it's gone, so I'm taking a day off for me."

"Good for you."

"Thanks."

"Can I get you anything?" Jackie and I were friendly, but not to the point of seeking each other out.

"I want to order two huge flower arrangements for the diner. One for each side of the counter."

"Fake?"

"Yes."

"What are you thinking?"

She shrugged. "I have no taste. What would you suggest?"

"Hmm." I tapped my fingers on the counter. "Roses. Daisies, maybe. Snapdragons are fun. I can mix a bunch of different things."

"That would be great. Can you have them ready in a week?"

"Sure. How big do you want them to be?"

"Oh, I don't know. About like this on the top." She opened her arms almost as wide as they would go.

"That's big."

"I want them to stand out."

"It'll cost about three hundred each."

"Three hundred? That's crazy!"

I shrugged. "They take a lot of time and materials if you want them to last." I was used to people balking at prices. They could take it or leave it. It didn't hurt my feelings.

"All right. I'm feeling careless today."

"What's put you in such a good mood?" I asked.

She shrugged. "Business is good, and nothing's threatening that anymore."

"Are you talking about Forrest?"

She grimaced. "I'm a bad person, aren't I? The poor guy dies, and I'm over the moon."

I didn't mention that she'd told me she didn't care about the winery. Apparently, she had.

"I doubt he would've made the winery a success. Forrest was full of ideas and not a lot of follow-through."

"I didn't mean to be insensitive. Sorry. I heard the two of you dated."

I rolled my eyes. "I don't know who started that rumor, but that's all it is. We went on one date—eighteen years ago." I was growing tired of saying it.

Jackie gave me a sympathetic smile and patted my hand. "That doesn't mean it doesn't hurt."

I laughed. "I feel bad about what happened, but I never had any feelings for him."

"That's not what everyone's saying."

"Great. That's all I need. People gossiping about me." I sighed.

"You know how it goes in small towns. They'll talk about you today and me tomorrow."

I nodded. "That seems to be the way. So what *is* everyone saying about me?"

"You really want to know?" She twirled the end of her braid between two fingers, waiting for me to consider it.

"Why not? There's nothing else to think about."

"Everyone's saying you and Forrest were practically engaged before he met Vivian. They say you hate her for stealing him."

I put my hands on my hips. "People really say that?"

"Yep."

"Ridiculous. I doubt we've spoken over three times since high school—and not much more before that. I thought he had a small crush on me, but I never felt the same.

"I wonder why everyone thinks things were different."

"Well, it's a new rumor, so I bet it's because Forrest died and everyone wants to say something about him."

She shook her head. "The rumor isn't new. I heard it about two months ago."

My eyes narrowed. "That's crazy. Who would start that? I'm never around him."

"People need things to talk about. They don't care if they have merit or not. I would judge, but I gossip plenty. People always want to gossip at the diner, and I admit, it makes the time pass quickly."

"I bet. I don't get a lot of people in here, but everyone tells me everything they know."

"Sometimes I wonder what people say about me. It's probably best I don't know."

I reassured her, "I've never heard anything too slanderous."

She threw back her head and laughed. "Good to know."

The door opened, and Troy walked in.

"Hi, Sheriff," Jackie said, smiling.

"Hello, Jackie. Neeley." Troy came up behind Jackie, and I told myself not to be jealous of her perfectly white smile. She was a little older than Troy, but still attractive.

"Do you need something?" I asked him.

"Go ahead and finish with Jackie. I've got time."

"We were just talking about how much gossip goes on in a small town," Jackie told him. "I bet you get to hear all of it."

Troy nodded. "I hear plenty. More about Crystal Rock than Clover Haven, though."

"You neglect us out here," she said, placing a hand on his arm. "You should split your time more evenly."

"Crystal Rock has more crime, so they need me more."

"I guess we'll have to change that, won't we, Neeley?" She rubbed Troy's arm, and he flinched.

I wanted to cringe at her flirting, but I just kept tapping on the counter. "Since you're here, can you do me a favor?" I asked him.

"Sure."

I moved around the counter and grabbed his free arm, tugging him away from Jackie. "The light fixture in the back needs a new bulb. There are spares in the closet."

"I'm on it." Troy hurried toward the back, and I sighed. I prided myself on being the kind of woman who changed her own lightbulbs, but I could tell he wanted to escape. Or maybe that was just wishful thinking.

Jackie gave me a sly smile. "It's like that, is it?"

"What are you talking about?"

"Everyone in town knows Neeley Kelter doesn't find a man to change her lightbulb. Are you and the sheriff a thing?"

My laugh came out more bitter than I intended. "Me and Troy? Never."

"I know you were a few years behind me in school, but you were with him all the time. At least, that's what I remember."

"Yeah, we've always been good friends." That always was a lie.

"So you've never been romantic?"

"Nope."

"Then it would be okay if I asked him out?"

I stared into her perfectly lined eyes, trying to think of a way to deter her without sounding like I cared.

I leaned forward and whispered, "He's... um... taken."

She raised a brow. "Oh?"

"He's keeping it quiet, because, you know. Small town."

"Ah. Got it. Well, I better be going." She spun around and called over her shoulder as she left, "Call me when the flowers are ready."

"I will." I took a relieved breath. I wasn't sure when I'd become a liar.

Troy came out. "None of the lights are burned out."

I grinned. "I know. I was saving you from Jackie."

"And I appreciate it. But what was with the, 'Me and Troy? Never?'" he asked, mimicking me in a high-pitched voice.

"Eavesdropper."

He laughed. "Guilty."

"Do you really want gossip running around about us?"

"If it keeps people like Jackie away, then yes."

"I did my best."

"You told her I'm taken. That's going to start rumors."

He had ears like an owl. "Sorry. Now you'll never get a date."

"Believe me, the women in Clover Haven do not tempt me."

I put my hands to my heart. "Ouch."

His lips curved. "You don't count. You're very tempting."

"It's too late. I'm already hurt." I held in a smile. I missed the back-and-forth I used to have with Troy and Chase.

He grabbed me around the waist and pulled me against him. "Don't be that way. Kiss me and you'll believe me."

I pulled away and laughed. "You wish."

He grinned. "I really do."

"Uh-huh. So, what brings you here?" I could joke all day about certain things, but I didn't want Troy teasing me about kissing. I couldn't let him know how much I would love that.

"Nothing good," he said, his smile fading. "The judge allowed the toxicology report, and it came back." He rubbed the back of his neck.

"And?"

"There was something in his system."

"Drugs?"

"No. They found something weird. Something called *datura*. They were vague on the details. Said they need to double-check something. I guess it can raise your heart rate and cause hallucinations."

I leaned against the high counter and clasped my hands in front of me. "Datura is a flower."

"Do you have any here?"

"No. They're also called devil's trumpet. Really toxic. I don't deal with things like that."

"What do they look like?"

"A bit like moonflowers."

"And those are the flowers that were on the table at the town hall?"

My stomach dropped, and a tingle ran up my spine. "Yes. They could be confused easily."

I turned and went out the front door. Troy followed close behind. I pointed at the flowerbeds. "Those are moonflowers."

They curled around the shop, though they were closed in the daylight. I'd planted other, brighter flowers in front of them to add color when the moonflowers weren't blooming.

"They'll climb anything if given the chance," I said. "Datura's more bushy."

We walked to the side, and I frowned when I spotted a bushy plant with broad, wavy leaves growing up between the moonflowers.

"What's wrong?" Troy asked. "You just went pale."

I pointed at the plant. "Datura looks like that."

"But that's a moonflower?"

"No."

He tilted his head. "What is it, then?"

"It looks like datura." I dropped to my hands and knees and pushed some of the moonflowers aside. "This has been here for a while. It's established and thriving."

"That's not good."

I brushed my side bangs from my eyes and looked up at him. "I swear I didn't plant these."

He held out his hands and pulled me to my feet. "Why would someone plant them here?"

"No one should. It doesn't make sense." My hands grew damp as my mind whirled with the consequences of what we'd discovered. "This is bad."

"I'm sure there's an explanation."

I shook my head. "Like what? It didn't spring up by itself. People are going to think I killed Forrest."

"I bet there are other plants around."

"I doubt it." I rubbed my arms. "I don't have time for this."

"For what?"

"Being accused of murder!"

Troy gave me a half smile. "No one has accused you of murder. You're overreacting."

"They will! I would, if it were someone else."

"Let's wait to panic until we have more to go on." He slid his arm around my shoulders and stared at the plant. "I might need to check around and see if it looks like someone's been tampering with things."

"How are you going to figure that out? I don't think fingerprints are going to show up on plants. This is insane! Someone must've planned this in advance. They planted it here and poisoned Forrest."

Troy hugged me and sighed. "I said no panicking. There has to be an explanation."

I tried to pull away, but he wasn't letting go. "If it were anyone else, you'd think they were guilty."

"Maybe. But I know you, I know you didn't do it."

I relaxed, trying not to focus on how intensely he was looking at me. "Everyone else will think it was me. What do we do?"

"You take care of Jackie's flowers," Troy said. "Let me handle this. Trust me, okay?"

I muttered something unintelligible and tried not to over-analyze the way he was looking at me.

But then—he leaned in.

It wasn't just in my head. He was definitely getting closer.

Troy was going to kiss me.

Why would he do that?

Maybe all these flowers really *were* making him hallucinate.

His phone rang, and he dropped his arms, shaking his head. He pulled it from his pocket and frowned. "Excuse me for a minute. I have to take this."

I rushed back into the shop.

That had been close. Too close. I couldn't imagine our friendship could survive anything new right now.

Chapter 6

I paced across my room and jumped when Murphy got in the way. "Whoa! Watch out, Murph." I picked him up and kept going. He put his paws over my shoulder and made a strange snorting sound in my ear. I grimaced but didn't stop walking.

"I think Troy was going to kiss me. It's good he got a phone call. He probably would've started avoiding me if it had happened. Maybe I'm just imagining things, why am I even worried about this? There are daturas in my garden that I didn't plant. That should be my worry."

Murphy squirmed, and I set him down. "Aren't you going to give me any advice?"

He ran in a circle and bumped into the wall.

"Nice move, Murph. I need a human friend to confide in, you don't give me anything to go on." I was sure Jessa and Roberta would listen, but I wasn't so sure they'd keep it to themselves.

"Okay, let's talk about what actually matters. Who put that plant in my flowers? No one is going to convince me they just popped up. The ones I cut for the meeting came from the front of the shop, and there's no datura there."

Murphy rolled over and rubbed his back against the carpet.

"I hope you don't have fleas. We don't have time for that."

I changed into my pajamas and pulled Troy's hoodie over my head. I probably should've given it back instead of wearing it and feeling sorry for myself all the time. I wasn't sure how I'd explain why I still had it. It wasn't like I stole it. He'd left it here, which was on him.

I climbed into bed and tried to think of anyone who might have something against me. I wasn't exciting enough to have many enemies. Whoever planted those flowers had to have done it with the intent to kill Forrest, and that meant they'd planned far in advance.

I ran through a list of people who might not like me, and a separate list of people who probably didn't like Forrest. None of them overlapped. I didn't know enough about Forrest to guess what most people thought of him, so my suspect list was limited to those who had spoken out against the winery.

The next morning, I rolled out of bed an hour later than usual. "Shoot!" I jumped up and was in and out of the shower in three minutes flat. I brushed through my long, dark hair, threw on a little makeup, and dashed off to the flower shop.

Roberta and Jessa were already in the back, busy putting things together. "Sorry I'm late."

"It's alright," Roberta said with a smug smile.

My eyes narrowed. "What's that look?"

"Nothing."

Jessa laughed. "I bet she's thinking about the rumors."

I rolled my eyes. "What rumors?"

Roberta's smile almost split her face. "The one about you and Sheriff Dreamy."

"We knew there wasn't anything to it," Jessa said, "but today at the diner, people were talking about you and the sheriff."

"Anything you want to confess?" Roberta teased.

"Nothing's happened."

"Jackie is saying she saw the two of you in the flower shop, kissing."

I wished. "Nope. No kissing. He hugged me. She must've exaggerated."

"Well, it's flying across town."

"Lovely."

"So... you and the sheriff have never kissed? Not in all those years you were friends?" Jessa asked.

"Never. Not even close. It wasn't like that. Ever." And I hated the fact.

"But he hugged you."

"I don't have to tell you how my grandpa is. Troy's parents weren't ever very affectionate, and our other friend Chase was raised by his aunt. We made a support group for ourselves. Lots of hugging, because we weren't getting that at home. Well, Chase's aunt hugged us all, but we got reliant on each other. It was never romantic."

"Too bad," Roberta said. "Someone around here needs romance."

"I volunteer you," I teased.

Roberta grinned. "I wish."

"There has to be someone desperate enough out there," Jessa teased.

Roberta tossed a stem at her, and they both burst into laughter.

"I'm thinking of building a small greenhouse," I said, changing the subject. "It would be fun to have our own flowers."

"Ooh," Roberta said. "That would be fun. I love planting things."

"I wonder if it would be worth it. I'm not sure how much we could grow, but we could start out small and see if it's something we can do."

"How small are we talking?" Jessa asked.

I paused to think for a moment. "About ten feet."

"That's not very big."

"No, but if it worked out well, I could build more."

"How hard is it?"

"I'm not sure. I just thought of it today, so I haven't spent much time on it."

Jessa grabbed a daisy. "Where would you put it?"

"I'm not sure. My grandpa owns all the land around here, and he doesn't do anything with it. I'll ask him if he minds."

"Do you want to hear a rumor even weirder than the one about you and the sheriff?"

"So long as it's not about me," I warned.

"No, it's about Vivian Cutler and Damion Burton."

Jessa groaned. "Not one of those kinds of rumors."

"It's an old rumor. When Forrest first brought Vivian to Clover Haven, they weren't fully committed. She was living in a rental."

Jessa nodded. "I remember that."

"Well, they agreed to date other people for a while, and during that time, Vivian and Damion were a thing."

I frowned. "I don't think something like that could've stayed quiet."

"They kept it under wraps. Forrest didn't even know. Damion really liked her, and he was upset when she chose Forrest."

"How did it come out?"

"Damion told his sister, and she stayed quiet—until Forrest died. Then she told someone, hoping Vivian might give Damion another chance. And that's all it took for the rumor to spread."

"Interesting," I said. "I wonder if Damion would talk about it?"

Jessa raised an eyebrow. "To you? I doubt it. I can't picture you chatting him up about relationship drama."

"Why not?"

"Have you ever talked to Damion?"

I shrugged. "Maybe. Just because I don't talk to everyone doesn't mean I can't. I just don't want to most of the time."

Roberta jumped in. "But why would you even want to talk to him about that? Seems a little weird."

I hesitated. "If I tell you, will you keep it between us?"

They both nodded.

"I think someone poisoned Forrest with a toxic flower."

They gasped in unison.

"Troy's trying to figure it out, but he's swamped. I thought it wouldn't hurt if I did a little asking around."

"Don't go questioning people who might be murderers," Jessa warned. "You never know what someone like that might do."

"I'll be careful," I promised.

"Who are your suspects?"

"I just added Damion. Then there's Jackie. She seems too happy about Forrest being gone. I might talk to Pedro, too—just because he didn't want the winery."

"Pedro isn't the type," Roberta said. "He's mellow."

"Maybe, but I'm going to talk to him. He was worried about his store. Am I missing anyone?"

"Anyone who might've hated Forrest? I would look into anyone who didn't want the winery. Including Jessa."

Jessa laughed. "You think I killed Forrest?"

"No. I'm just saying you might look a little suspicious."

"I guess. I didn't want the winery, that's for sure. Has the sheriff searched Forrest's house to see if anything was strange?"

"I'm not sure. All I know is that something was in Forrest's blood. I don't know what else has been figured out. Do you know Vivian's schedule?" I asked. "I could go search right now if she isn't home."

"She flew to her parents'," Jessa said. "She won't be back for three days."

"Great. Anyone want to come?"

"I do!" Roberta said, raising her hand.

Jessa shook her head. "Not me. I'm not getting arrested for breaking and entering. I'll watch the shop."

Roberta and I arrived at the Cutler home fifteen minutes later. It wasn't huge, but it was nice. It was an old farmhouse that had been completely remodeled. The house was two stories, with a wraparound porch, and every window had large shutters. The white paint was fresh, and the wooden door looked new. I immediately spotted the ivy climbing gently up the porch railing, where a wooden swing creaked in the breeze as we pulled up.

"Now what?" Roberta asked as we got out of the car. "I bet it's locked. I can open an easy door with a credit card, but I'm guessing they don't have that kind of door."

"Probably not."

We went up the four steps to the porch, and I tried the knob. Locked. "Let's try the back." It was also locked.

"What are you two doing?"

I spun around to see Troy standing there, hands on his hips.

I gave an awkward curtsy. "Hello, Sheriff."

He tipped his cowboy hat. "Ma'am."

Roberta snorted. "It was less strange when you two weren't friends."

I laughed. "We were seeing if Vivian was home."

"She's not. Why are you at the back door?"

I shared a look with Roberta.

She shrugged. "We were making sure she locked her doors, since she didn't seem to be home. We wouldn't want anyone to break in."

"I see. It's good you two aren't criminals. You'd be terrible at it. I've never seen two people look so guilty, and I see guilty people all the time."

I tilted my head. "I don't feel guilty. You just scared me."

"I hope you two weren't going to go inside."

I gave him my best smile. "I seriously doubt we'd admit it to you if we were."

He smiled. "Come on. I'll buy you both lunch."

I sighed, and the three of us walked toward the diner, which wasn't too far away. It was early for lunch, but Troy could eat anytime.

When we got to the diner, Troy took off his hat, and I smirked at his hat hair. I reached up and ran my hands through it. It didn't make it neater, but it looked better than pasted to his head.

"Am I presentable?" he joked.

"Almost."

Someone seated us and brought water. I sat next to Roberta and across from Troy.

Troy took a sip. "What were you two actually doing at the Cutlers'?"

My lips twitched. "We really were trying the doorknobs to make sure they were locked."

"What were you going to do if they weren't?"

Roberta giggled. "We plead the fifth."

Troy nodded. "Mm-hmm. That's what I thought."

"Hey," I said, pointing my napkin-bound silverware at him. "Don't judge us. What were you doing there?"

"My job."

"That's what we were doing. Your job."

He sighed. "Come on, Neeley. I've got this."

"I'm sure you do."

"No breaking into people's houses." He eyed me, a look I knew meant he was serious about this.

I redirected, "Have you searched it?"

He leaned against the booth. "Not yet."

"I bet that's what you were about to do. Take us with you."

He shook his head. "I can't, you know that. I hope you won't go back."

Roberta held up her hands. "Not me. You almost gave me a heart attack when you came up behind us."

He raised his brows. "Neeley?"

"Yes?"

"You aren't going back, right?"

"Probably not. How will I know if you do a thorough job, though?"

"I'll do just fine."

"Do you want to get together later and compare suspects?" I asked.

He leaned forward, his elbows on the table. "I'll find you this evening."

"I should be home."

Roberta rolled up her straw wrapper. "Is Forrest's body at the mortuary?"

"No," Troy said. "When we think there might be something suspicious, we send them into the city so we can run more tests."

"That's good. I'd hate to think someone in town might be sneaking around in the mortuary with Neeley there, trying to ruin any evidence."

I smiled at my friend. "You watch too many movies."

"I sure do."

Chapter 7

"Did you find any clues?" Jessa asked when we returned to the shop.

"We didn't even get in," I said. "It was a waste of time."

"You were gone for a while."

Roberta giggled. "We had to eat lunch with the sheriff so he and Neeley could flirt."

"We were not flirting," I protested.

"Oh please, I know flirting when I see it."

"I should've been there," Jessa said. "What happened?"

Roberta grinned. "Neeley ran her hands through his hair, then they kept teasing each other."

I rolled my eyes. "I was fixing his hat hair."

"Hmm. I was almost certain you were going to pull him in for a kiss. I bet you would've if you'd been alone."

"No. That's just the way our relationship is."

Jessa shook her head. "But it could be better. You should've pulled him in."

"You two are crazy. It isn't like that with us. We did have to promise we wouldn't go to Vivian's house. But I am going to go back to the diner sometime. I'm not sure I trust Jackie." I paused and then asked, "Did anyone come in while we were gone?"

"Billie came and got a bouquet. She sure spends a lot on flowers."

"Did she complain about the price?"

"Of course. She said she might stop buying roses if they don't get cheaper."

I smiled. "She says that about once a month, and she keeps buying them. If everyone in Clover Haven bought as many flowers as Billie, we'd be raking in the dough."

"I cleaned everything up," Jessa said. "I need to go up to the mortuary."

"Go ahead. I'll lock up."

Jessa grabbed her purse and left.

"When are you going to the diner?" Roberta asked.

"After it closes and everyone leaves. Do you want to come?"

"Nope. It scared me enough when the sheriff caught us earlier."

I was secretly relieved. Only worrying about myself would make things easier. I locked up and went home. Having rushed through my duties at the mortuary, I then devoted my time to playing games with Murphy on the floor.

A knock came at my bedroom door.

"Come in."

Troy entered quietly and sat across from me. Murphy ran to him and curled up on his lap. Lucky dog.

"Are you going to tell me your list of suspects?"

I smiled. "Are you going to tell me yours?"

"Nope."

"I figured. Jackie's still at the top of my list. Then I've got two maybe-suspects I haven't ruled out: Damion and Pedro."

"Interesting," Troy said, rubbing Murphy's back like he wasn't aware of the string of drool soaking into his pants.

"You can probably cross off Damion," he added.

"Oh?"

"He's been dating someone he met online for a few months. They're on a cruise. They left at least two weeks ago."

"So he couldn't have poisoned Forrest from the Lido deck."

"Exactly. I even double-checked to make sure he actually got on the ship. I knew about his history with Vivian."

I watched the dark, shiny wet spot on Troy's jeans spread like an oil spill. "I didn't know dogs drooled so much until I got Murphy."

"Some breeds are worse. You'll build up a tolerance."

"I move him when he starts to melt on me. I have boundaries."

Troy grinned. "Guess I'm immune to gross dog stuff."

"I should take a course. Like 'What to Expect When You're Experiencing Drool.' I'm winging it."

"You can Google anything," he said, patting Murphy's head.

"I'm building a greenhouse."

"That's a jump in topics."

"I contain multitudes."

He laughed. "Need help?"

"I'll manage."

"Chase and I worked construction for a while. We could be handy."

"I'll let you know. If it goes well, maybe I'll let you help me build a house someday."

His brow lifted. "You're building a house now?"

"Not yet. But I've always lived at the mortuary. Sometimes I think I'd like my own cozy little place without embalming fluid in the air."

"I'd be glad to help."

Murphy let out a dramatic sigh, drool stringing from his jowls to Troy's knee.

Troy's phone dinged, so he read the message and groaned. "Dang. I was hoping to sleep tonight."

"You don't usually?"

"Usually. Not always. Something's going on in Crystal Rock."

"Can't someone else go?"

"I could send someone, but I like having eyes on things there. Crime's been picking up." He stood and handed Murphy to me like he was passing off a wet bag of laundry. "I'll talk to you later," he said.

I nodded and watched him leave. It was probably for the best. That meant I could go search the diner. I wasn't sure what time customers would clear out or when the staff would finish for the night, so I waited until it had been closed for two hours. I figured that gave the cleaning crew time to come and go.

I thought about wearing black, but that would look more suspicious if someone saw me, so I settled for jeans and a brown shirt. I put gloves in my pocket and took the back way around town, approaching the diner from behind.

All the lights were off—at least from the back. I tried the back door. It was locked, but it wasn't a fancy lock, and it was old. I hated to admit it, but I'd popped plenty of locks in my day. My grandpa was always locking doors in the morgue that he didn't want disturbed, and that had made me curious. Troy, Chase, and I had opened every door we'd been locked out of.

For my fifteenth birthday, Chase had given me a decompression tool I could use to pick locks.

Now, I pulled the very same tool from my pocket. It looked like a pocket knife, but everything that opened up was something that could be used in different locks.

I fumbled around with the knob. I'd gotten rusty. Now that I wasn't a nosy teenager, I hadn't picked a lock in ages. It took five minutes, but I finally got it. The door creaked open, and I stepped inside.

Since the kitchen was at the back of the diner, it was safe to flip on the light. No one would notice unless they came around back, and there wasn't a reason for that.

The kitchen was spotless. Two large ovens took up one corner, and a big stovetop stretched across one side of the room. My shoes clicked against the tan tiles, but who was going to hear me? It didn't take long to get bored. I opened everything and looked inside, only to find ingredients and kitchen tools.

I'd searched almost all the cupboards, except one that was too high to reach. A yawn cracked my jaw, and I figured it was probably time to go home. Still... if I didn't check the last cupboard, I'd always wonder.

I grabbed a stool and climbed up, opening the cupboard. It was full of tablecloths. My brows drew together as I pulled them out. In the back corner was a small canister. It was probably full of something boring, but I had to know. I grabbed it and unscrewed the lid, wrinkling my nose. The smell was awful—like old leaves, almost moldy, and strangely chemical all at once.

I shook the container. It appeared to be dried leaves. The wavy edges and broad shape made me think of the datura flower. I could've been imagining it because that was on my mind. It might've been sage or basil. It sure didn't smell like it, though.

I returned the canister to its place and jumped down from the stool. I scanned the kitchen, making sure I had left no sign of being there. When I was satisfied, I flipped off the lights and left, locking the door behind me.

Now to decide what to do. Calling Troy would be the smart thing, but he was busy with something else. It was doubtful anyone would move the canister before tomorrow. If they had wanted to, they could have by now.

I decided to go home and deal with it in the morning. I stopped when I was almost out of the main part of town. I wasn't far from Vivian's house. There wasn't much reason to go snooping there, since I was almost positive Jackie and her dried leaves were guilty.

I sighed. This was just like checking my locks multiple times. I'd be bothered unless I at least walked by. Changing directions, I headed toward the Cutler house. Vivian might be back any day, and I wanted to see if Forrest had left any clues as to why someone would kill him. The obvious answer was the winery, but to just assume would be narrow-minded.

The moon guided me. Very few people in Clover Haven left their porch lights on. I'd overheard someone say Troy encouraged people to start, but folks here were stubborn. When I reached Vivian's house, it was completely dark.

This would be the second time I used my lock pick tonight.

I took the doorknob, and before I could do anything, the door opened a few inches. My eyes narrowed, and I pushed it. It had been locked the last time I was here, and I doubted Vivian was back. Troy might've gone in and forgotten to check the locks when he left, but I doubted that, too.

I stepped into the doorway and held still for a moment, listening. All I could hear were crickets behind me. I counted to one hundred, then entered, inaudibly closing the door. Turning on the lights would be a big flag for anyone walking by, so I turned on my phone's flashlight. I'd never been in here before, and I didn't want to risk hurting myself in the dark. In front of me was a staircase, and a hallway ran along the side of it. I hoped Forrest had an office, because that was probably where anything important would be. I moved through the main floor. It had a living room, kitchen, bathroom, and dining room. Nothing caught my attention, so I went up the carpeted stairs. At the top, the hallway went in two directions. I turned right and went into the first room I came to.

"Bingo," I muttered. I'd found the office. A computer desk sat against one wall, with a computer on top. I sat on the edge of the chair and stared at the bright screen.

I hadn't expected Forrest's computer to be on. The page that was open appeared to be an email. I wouldn't normally read an email that wasn't mine, but I had questions.

Hey Forrest,
Do we have a deal? What was the outcome of the meeting? I need to jump on this, so are you in or out?
Tim

"Hmm. Who is Tim?" I awkwardly used my gloves to go to Forrest's inbox. Nothing else caught my eye. I froze when I heard a small sound behind me. I grabbed my phone and turned, shining the light on a closet door. My heart skipped a beat, then shot into full panic mode. There was nothing in the closet. I was just freaking myself out. Still, I didn't move for a full minute.

Then another small noise reached my ear. I stood and walked to the closet. I touched the knob—and it suddenly flew open.

Someone burst out, knocking me to the ground. I jumped up and bolted after the dark figure. There was nothing graceful about my exit. I hit my shoulder on the way out and stumbled as I turned the corner. I could hardly see, but the person I chased was making plenty of noise as they took the stairs three at a time. I grabbed the rail and ran down as fast as I could. Several questions ran through my mind. One: why was I chasing someone who might be dangerous? Two: why hadn't I told people where I was going? And three: why don't I carry a weapon? The person crashed into the front door, and I slammed into their back. "Stop!" I yelled.

The man pushed me back and opened the door.

I slammed into him again, sending him tumbling onto the porch. He looked up at me, and my mouth turned down.

"Pedro?"

He took a deep breath and tilted his head. "Neeley? Is that you? What are you doing in Forrest's house?"

I put my hands on my hips. "What are *you* doing in Forrest's house?"

He sighed and got to his feet. "Forrest told me he had a partner for the winery. I thought I might be able to come here and figure out who it was."

"Why would you need to know?"

He might've shrugged, but it was pretty dark. "If I know who it is, I can research them and see if they might still open a winery. It's possible they don't have the resources without Forrest, but I want to know what I'm up against."

"Do you really sell so much alcohol it would hurt your store?"

"Yes. Now, are you going to tell me why *you* were here?"

I wasn't about to say I needed to make sure I didn't get thrown in jail for Forrest's murder. "I thought Forrest might've been up to something. I just wanted to see if there was anything pointing to that."

"Did you see the email?"

"Yes."

"I pulled it up. I bet Tim is the partner he talked about. The problem is, there are a lot of Tims out there."

I nodded into the darkness. "True."

"Are you going to tell anyone I was here?"

"Depends. Are you going to tell anyone I was here?"

"No."

"Sorry I knocked you over." Pedro wasn't what I'd call old, but he was over fifty, and a fall might not be in his best interest.

"It's fine. Now I'm going to go home and pretend this didn't happen."

I laughed softly. "Good idea."

Chapter 8

"Neeley! Wake up!" Grandpa pounded on my door.

With a groan, I climbed out of bed, wobbled to the door, and opened it a crack. "What's wrong?"

"The Morton funeral, it's tonight."

"And?"

"The Mortons didn't exactly plan in advance. They were down at your shop to order flowers."

My eyes went wide. "For tonight?"

"Yes. I told them you would be right down."

I threw my arms in the air. "You want me to prepare flowers for a funeral *tonight*?"

"They're distraught. I hope you will."

I took a deep breath. "I'll do my best, but it's going to be bad if they're picky. If they'll go with what I have, I can pull it off."

"Thanks."

Murphy barked from where he lay on the corner of my bed. I got dressed in record time and hurried down to the shop, Murphy at my heels.

A woman about sixty stood near the door, tapping her foot. She put me in mind of Aunt Marge from the *Harry Potter* movie. When she saw me, she pointed her thick finger at me. "How do you stay in business if you aren't here?" She might've had the look and the personality, too.

I tried to remain calm. "The shop opens at nine. It's seven."

"My father's funeral is tonight, and we need to get the flowers ordered."

I pulled out a key and opened the shop. She pushed past me, and I frowned. She was having a hard day, so I let it pass. Murphy ran in after her and into the back room. He knew where I hid his treats.

"This has to be breathtaking," she said. "I need everyone to remember it. I want all white and red roses. We need at least two big bouquets for the sides of the casket—and something to go on top. Then we need a bunch for the hallways that people walk down to get to the funeral."

"I'm sorry, but I don't carry that many roses."

She glared at me. "That's unprofessional."

"Most people order things like this in advance. I can't have that much inventory in the store unless I know it's needed, or it all goes bad."

"Humph. Ridiculous."

I was tired from my late night, but this woman had just lost her father. I wasn't about to launch into a lecture about how pointless it would be for me to carry that many white and red roses regularly.

"I can make something nice, but only if you aren't too choosy. I normally have a few days' notice to get things. The day of, there's no way I can get that many roses. I can only use what I have."

"Maybe I'll take my business elsewhere."

"You do what you have to, but I'm the only flower shop in the county. If you go to the city, they're going to tell you the same thing. Flower shops can't keep large inventory for long."

"Why not?"

I held in an eye roll. "Because once a flower is cut, it starts to die. And since this is a small town, we don't get many calls for big orders, so we need them placed in advance."

"Fine. Do what you can, but I expect a heavy discount."

"Why?"

"Because you aren't giving me what I want."

I pursed my lips and held in a retort. "I'm sorry, but I can't give a discount because you didn't plan ahead."

"Ahead? How was I to know my father would die when he did?"

"His funeral has been scheduled for over a week. If you had called then—"

"I'm not going to argue with you. The funeral director is a friend of mine. He isn't going to like the way you're treating me. I bet he'll break off any agreements he has with your shop."

I rolled my eyes. I couldn't hold it in anymore. "Before you say anything that might make you seem more ridiculous, my grandfather is the funeral director."

Her nostrils flared. "How much do I owe you?" she asked through gritted teeth.

"Tell me everything you need."

She listed it off, and I wrote the prices as she went. When she finished, I showed her the total.

"Ridiculous. Who pays that much for flowers?"

"Everyone who buys flowers. I'm going to have to sit here all day trying to get this ready—because *you* weren't prepared."

"You're taking advantage of people dying." Her face had grown red, her brows drawn.

"There's no requirement that says a funeral needs flowers."

"Flowers are cheap. You're marking it up."

"I have to make a profit."

"Just for putting some flowers together? That should be free."

"Do you have a job?"

"Of course I do. I teach fifth grade."

I gave a terse smile. "How lucky for those children. It doesn't cost you anything to teach, so maybe you should do it for free."

"That doesn't make sense."

"Neither does the fact that you want me to do this without making any money. It's my job. If I only charged you the price of the flowers, I'd spend all day working for you and make nothing. Besides, you made me come in early, and it's going to put me behind on everything else I have to do today."

She tossed her debit card at me, and I ran it through. Then she stomped away, and I sighed in relief. This wasn't how I wanted to spend my day. I couldn't even call Jessa or Roberta. I'd left so fast, I'd forgotten my phone.

I went to the back and started grabbing supplies and placing them on the table. Just because poor Mr. Morton's daughter wasn't pleasant didn't mean he shouldn't have nice flowers for his funeral. I pulled up my sleeves and got to work.

❦

"Are we going to make it?" Jessa asked, sticking a sparkling ribbon into the arrangement she was working on.

I nodded. "Just barely. Miss Morton will be here to pick it up in fifteen minutes."

The morning had passed too quickly, and we'd already missed lunch.

"Are you going to the social tonight?" Roberta asked as she placed a rose in a bouquet.

"Nope."

"You never go."

"I don't see a reason."

"You get to mingle with all the people in town. They usually have good refreshments. And there's the dance. Someday, I swear a handsome man is going to move to town and find me at the monthly social."

I smiled. "I'm sure it'll happen."

I'd been to exactly one town social in the last ten years. I didn't date because I chose not to date. Going to the social made every man in town think you were announcing your availability. Families had a great night, but being single, there was a circus. I knew every single man who lived in Clover Haven and didn't want to encourage any of them.

"I'm going," Jessa said. "It's fun. You should try it."

"I've tried it. I don't want to dance with anyone in town." I picked up another flower.

"You don't have to dance."

"But then I have to tell people no, and that's awkward."

Roberta snipped a ribbon. "You could dance and still have fun. I'm not interested in anyone here, but I enjoy it anyway."

Jessa nodded. "Me too. And tonight the sheriff's coming. The mayor asked him to, since people are on edge. Now that word's gotten out that Forrest was poisoned, everyone's nervous."

I kept my eyes fixed on the flowers in front of me. Maybe I would let them talk me into it. I couldn't let them know it was because of Troy.

"I would go if I didn't have to dance."

"We can spread it around that you don't want to dance."

"And you think that will help?"

"It might."

By the time the flowers were picked up, I was happy with what we'd accomplished. The flowers might not all be roses, but they were pretty. I hoped they wouldn't mind that some of the arrangements were fake. Those usually cost more, but I hadn't charged extra.

Jessa had to leave for her receptionist job, and Roberta and I stayed to catch up on everything we'd fallen behind on because of the funeral. By the time we finished, I was in no mood for a social.

I went to my room with my hyper dog and sat on the bed. "I don't need to go to the social, right?"

Murphy ignored me and went to his water dish.

"There probably aren't many women who would want to dance with Troy—"

Murphy turned his head and barked.

"You're right. Everyone will want to dance with him. He's the sheriff, though, so maybe he won't dance." I looked at my nightstand. My phone wasn't where I usually charged it. I must've left it in the kitchen last night.

"I guess I could go for a minute." I loved having a dog. It made me feel less crazy when I talked to myself. I could pretend the dog was listening.

I wasn't wearing a dress—that would look like I was trying to catch someone's eye. I changed into a cute green shirt and ran a brush through my hair.

I wasn't a vain person, but I loved my hair. People complained about straight or curly hair not doing what they wanted, but mine usually looked good no matter what I did. If I curled it, it stayed nice for three days. If I slept on it wet, I brushed it and it was shiny and straight the next day.

"I'm going out. Are you alright without me? Grandpa has a funeral, so he can't entertain you."

Murphy went to his bed and flopped over. I guessed that was a yes.

Normally I'd walk the mile, but not today. I got into my car and drove to the Bentleys' barn. They rotated locations for these things, but barns were always a favorite. I understood the charm, but no matter what you did to a barn, it was still going to smell.

I parked on the road along with a long line of cars and walked around to the back. Music spilled from the inside, and I forced myself to head toward it. I'd find Roberta and Jessa and stay hidden in a corner.

A lot of people came just to talk, so there were plenty of small groups sitting in circles, and five couples dancing. I frowned when I noticed one of them was Troy—Troy and Kellie Parker.

I didn't have anything against Kellie, but she was way too young for Troy. Okay, maybe only four years, but she wasn't his type.

She tossed her curly blond hair and laughed at something he said. I hoped she wasn't the woman he'd been in love with.

I scanned the room for my friends, and my eyes landed on Pedro. I frowned. I hadn't seen my phone since he'd bumped into me. My eyes went wide...

My phone was in Forrest Cutler's home office. How was I supposed to explain that? And I still hadn't told Troy about the dried flowers at the diner.

I didn't believe in cutting in on a dance. It was rude and said you thought you were more important than the person they were already with. That was my stance—but I was throwing it out the window.

I hurried across the dance floor and tapped Kellie on the shoulder. "Can I cut in?"

She glared at me. "No, you—"

"Thanks," I said, already pushing her aside.

Troy's eyes went wide as I put my arms around his neck. Kellie stomped away, and Troy placed his hands on my waist.

I pressed my cheek to his and whispered in his ear, "My phone is in Forrest Cutler's home office."

He pulled me closer, if that was possible, and whispered back, "Do I want to know why?"

"Probably not."

"I'll go get it."

"There's more."

Troy smelled good. He almost blocked out the barn smell. I wanted to run my hands over his arms, but I'd probably caused enough gossip as it was.

"What?" he asked.

"Hmm?"

"What else did you need to tell me?"

"Oh, right. There's a cupboard in the diner that's up high. It's full of tablecloths. In the back, there's a canister full of some kind of dried plant. I think it's datura."

"Dang it, Neeley. You're going to get yourself into trouble." His lips brushed my ear, and I shivered.

"Probably." I kissed his cheek and released him, then made a beeline for the dessert table.

Roberta waved at me, so I grabbed a cup of water and headed over.

"You came!" Roberta said.

I nodded and fanned my face. "It's hot in here."

"Not really," she said with a sly wink. "That conversation you were having with the sheriff looked hot, though."

I rolled my eyes. "I told you. We're good friends."

"You kissed him."

I shrugged. "On the cheek." I was only lying to myself. I'd hugged Troy a million times, but that was the first time my lips had touched him. I should probably avoid him. Who knew what I'd do next?

"What was that all about?" Jessa asked, pushing her way over to us.

"Nothing," I said. I might've caused some serious damage here.

"Nothing? I thought you were going to start making out on the dance floor."

"I had to tell him something important. It wasn't romantic at all, but I couldn't let anyone hear. I'll tell you about it later when there aren't so many people around."

"Is it about Forrest?"

I nodded.

Kellie joined our group and glared at me. "Why did you scare the sheriff off?"

"I didn't."

"Then why did he take off after your ridiculous little display?"

"Because he has things to do?"

"He told me he was staying until the end."

"I'm not sure why it's any of your business."

"I was dancing with him! It's rude to cut in. People don't do that anymore."

"It was an emergency."

"What?" Her brown eyes shot daggers. "You needed to whisper sweet nothings in his ear?"

I turned to my friends. "I'm going to leave."

Kellie crossed her arms. "Why? To meet the sheriff?"

Jessa raised her brow. "So what if she is?"

Kellie muttered something under her breath and stormed away. No one messed with Jessa. She had an intimidating presence when she wanted to.

"I'm not meeting him," I said. "I just hate these things. I'll see you tomorrow, alright?"

"Stay for thirty minutes," Roberta begged.

I sighed. "Fine. Thirty minutes."

Chapter 9

I sank into a chair and took a deep breath. The square dance was killer. I'd only danced it because Jim asked me, and he wasn't a threat to my weird way of life. For being sixty-four, he sure could move.

I'd been at the dance for more than the thirty minutes I promised, but I'd started having fun against my will.

Troy had appeared a while later, his eyes scanning the room. When they landed on me, he made his way over and tossed me my phone.

I caught it. "Thanks."

He nodded. His lips were pressed into a thin line, and I wondered what he was thinking. I tried to come up with something normal to say, but all I could think about was kissing his cheek.

He didn't look happy, and I worried I might be the reason. What if he was trying to think of a way to tell me I shouldn't have done that? He was the sheriff; he had a reputation to uphold.

He sat in the chair next to me and watched the couples dance by.

"Troy?"

"Hmm?" He didn't look at me.

"I'm sorry about earlier. I didn't realize how bad that all looked."

"What are you talking about?"

"On the dance floor?"

"Don't worry about it. I'm sure no one thought anything."

"Roberta and Jessa seem to think otherwise. I know you have a reputation to uphold. I hope I didn't damage it."

He glanced over and gave me one of his famous Troy smiles. "You know I don't care about gossip."

"Well, I should've told you somewhere more private."

His smile faded. "Believe me, that would've been worse."

"Right. I guess the sheriff can't go running out of a barn dance with someone."

Troy shook his head and turned back to the crowd.

"I'm also sorry I cut in on your dance. Kellie's not happy with me."

"Kellie doesn't drive me as crazy as some, but I was happy for the interruption."

At his words, a surprising warmth filled my chest. But I couldn't think too much about it, so asked, "Did you check the diner?"

"I can't without a warrant or Jackie's permission."

"She might let you. If she doesn't, she'll know she looks guilty."

"I guess that's true."

"She's right over there," I said, pointing.

He stood and made his way across the room.

Jessa took his seat. "You're killing the sheriff, honey."

I laughed. "What are you talking about?"

"You *know* he has a thing for you. You should've seen his face when you were whispering to him earlier. And now he's all quiet and broody. That's because he knows you're a man-hater."

"Come on, Jessa. I'm not a man-hater."

"You don't hate *that* one. Anyone can see that. So do something about it."

"We're only friends. That's how we've always been." I shrugged, feeling like a broken record.

"Have you asked him if he wants more?"

"Of course not. We have the same kind of friendship we've always had."

"Then you've always had a dysfunctional relationship."

I smiled. "You're crazy."

"Sometimes, but I think I'm right about this. You grab the sheriff and give him a kiss, and he's gonna kiss you right back."

My heart had started pounding, and I tried to shake it off. "It's not going to happen." But I secretly wondered what Troy would do if I kissed him. He'd probably stop coming to Clover Haven, and I'd never see him again.

"Alright. Whatever you say." Was that disappointment in her tone?

I watched Troy talk to Jackie. She was smiling and nodding. The two of them walked over to me.

"I've given Sheriff McGregor permission to search the diner," Jackie said. "I just want to make sure there are witnesses."

Troy nodded. "Thanks, Jackie."

She handed him a key and went back to what she was doing.

"I'm leaving," I said, getting to my feet. "It's been a long day."

Troy nodded. "I'll walk you to your car. Have a good evening, Jessa."

I didn't turn back to see whatever look Jessa was giving me. "I'm shocked Jackie was so agreeable," I said.

"I told her I need to search anyone's place who might have anything against Forrest. She understood. She didn't seem worried at all."

"That's odd. You should probably hurry over so she doesn't run there and move anything."

"She didn't look like she was going to leave anytime soon."

"Do you want me to come with you and show you where it is?"

"No. I think I can figure it out. You should go home and sleep."

"Wait. There's something else I forgot to tell you. I pretty much implied I wouldn't say anything, but it could be important."

"I'm listening."

"When I went to Forrest's, I was reading his email."

Troy smiled and shook his head. "Of course you were. You should meet Chase's wife. You two have a lot in common. She can't stay out of other people's business either."

I ignored him. "I didn't learn much from the email, except Forrest might've had a partner for the winery. When I was reading it, I heard something in the closet. It turns out Pedro was in there."

He rubbed his chin. "In the closet?"

"Yes. He said he was trying to figure out who Forrest's partner was, so he'd know if he should feel threatened. But what if he was trying to find out who it was so he could kill the partner? What if he killed Forrest?"

Troy's brows came together. "Pedro? I have a hard time believing he could be a killer."

"I don't see him as a violent killer, but maybe poison."

"I thought you were convinced it was Jackie."

"I am—for the most part. But I could be completely wrong. She might have a container of basil, for all I know. I think the leaves were too big for that, though. I just don't want to lock onto one idea and ignore everything else that might be important."

Troy left in his truck, and I drove home. Pedro's excuse still felt weak to me. It sounded like something someone would say because they'd been caught. Troy was right, though. Pedro seemed like a nice guy.

It was after ten when I got home, so I got ready for bed and made sure the morgue was clean. We had a part-time housekeeper, but sometimes that wasn't enough. I checked on Grandpa and frowned when I saw Murphy sleeping at the foot of his bed. I went in quietly and scooped him up.

When we got to my room, I poured him some food, which he ignored. Grandpa must've fed him already.

I felt so much more rested the next day. Murphy came with me to the flower shop, and I ordered more flowers. We'd used a lot yesterday and, thankfully, had heard no complaints from the funeral patrons.

Thinking about the greenhouse, I decided I also wanted to make a small fenced area behind the shop for Murphy. He'd do well with more outside time, but he didn't strike me as the kind of dog who'd enjoy being too far from people.

"You missed all the excitement last night," Jessa told me as she entered the shop with Roberta.

"Oh yeah?"

"The sheriff came into the dance and asked to see Jackie. They went outside to talk, and I don't know what happened, but he arrested her. Everyone stayed extra late speculating about it."

Roberta nodded. "No one knows why he arrested her, but I figure it has to be related to Forrest Cutler."

"I didn't tell you two what happened the other night. I'll give you the fast version. I broke into Jackie's diner and found a canister with strange dried leaves. I think it might be what someone used to drug Forrest."

"Then it was her," Jessa said.

"Maybe. It looks possible. That's what I was telling Troy last night at the dance. It's more complicated, though. I also snuck into Forrest and Vivian's house. Pedro was there."

Roberta put her hands to her cheeks. "Why would he be there?"

"It's hard to know."

"I'd blame Jackie over Pedro."

Jessa snickered. "That's because he danced with you twice last night."

Roberta punched her playfully on the arm. "That's not the only reason. He's a nice guy."

I moved the flowers in front of me. "He told me the winery might really hurt his business. That's motive."

"Yes, but the sheriff arrested Jackie, so it was probably her."

"Probably," I agreed.

I wished I could go talk to Troy. He was likely in Crystal Rock. Now that he had Jackie in custody, he might not be back for a while.

"Are we ready for book club tonight?" Roberta asked. "We could cancel. Everyone's probably too distracted about Jackie to pay attention."

"Let's not cancel," Jessa protested. "I don't have a lot to look forward to these days, book club is my escape."

Murphy sneezed in the back room, then came running out. His cute little flat face was covered in yellow powder.

"What are you into?" I asked, kneeling down and brushing off his face. He sneezed all over my arms and I jumped up. "Gross. I think someone's been sticking their face in the peonies." He sneezed again.

"I'm thinking of putting in a small fence in the back so he can play outside."

Roberta grabbed a tissue and tried to clean his face. "Good idea. I think he gets bored in here all day."

"I would leave him with my grandpa, but then he doesn't get his work done. For a person who refused to have animals all his life, Grandpa sure likes Murphy. He spoils him when I'm not looking. When they're together, I always come home and smell bacon or hamburger on his breath."

"You're planning a lot of projects," Jessa said.

"I know. I need to actually do some of them and stop planning. I bought a greenhouse kit, so I can start on that as soon as it comes."

"You can get a greenhouse kit?" Jessa asked.

Roberta nodded. "You can get a kit for just about anything these days. What will you plant in the greenhouse?"

"I'm not sure. Since roses seem to be one of the most popular things, I'm thinking of planting them around the morgue. I'll save the greenhouse for plants that are a little more finicky. Probably things like zinnias, marigolds, and orchids."

Jessa arched an eyebrow. "I thought you were against marigolds?"

"I am. I think they're the smelliest flower. Just thinking about them gives me allergies. But I've had people request them a lot lately. I don't understand it, but if it's what the customer wants, then what can I do?"

"Orchids are hard to grow," Roberta said. "Every time I get one, it looks nice for a couple of months, then the flower dies and never comes back."

"That's why a greenhouse might be nice. Some flowers like humidity and more heat. We can control it better. I might just be adding another thing that'll be annoying to deal with, but it could be fun."

There was never enough time in the day, but Jessa was right. I needed to stop planning and start doing.

Chapter 10

"This book made me hungry!" Jim said. "I'm not sure I can handle all these culinary mysteries we keep reading. I sit, read, and eat."

"That's why I made my scones!" Patty said, motioning to the table.

"Yay!" Roberta said, picking up a scone and grabbing the honey butter. "Way to stick to the theme, Patty."

I picked up my copy of *And Then There Were Scones.* Matilda Swift's mystery definitely made a person want a scone.

"I knew I was going to like the book as soon as I saw the author was from England," Patty said. "British authors know how to do it right."

"They aren't all good," Billie said. "You can't decide to like a book because of where the author is from."

"Sure I can," Patty insisted. "I do it all the time. And it was a good book."

"Yes, but you didn't know that until you read it."

"I love books about baking competitions," Lydia said, cutting in. "My dream would be to be in one. I don't want to get blamed for a murder like poor Jessica."

"Just like poor Jackie," Billie said.

"Poor Jackie?" Patty said. "She got arrested for murder."

"But what are the chances she's innocent?"

"Small. You've been reading too many books. Sometimes the guilty person is just guilty. The sheriff found evidence in her kitchen."

I frowned and drummed my fingers on the table. Was the evidence at the diner any worse than the evidence in my garden? The dreaded flowers were growing right next to my moonflowers. Troy hadn't said anything about that since we discovered them. Still, I was almost sure he'd looked around when I wasn't there.

I needed to ask him. Once he allowed it, I would tear them all out and plant something else.

"So, back to Jessica," Jim said. "We know she has a good grip because she whisks things so much. That was something I haven't read before that I found amusing."

"Whisking is no joke," I said. "I can do it for a minute, but man. I don't have whisking muscles. I usually pull out the mixer."

"I can't wait to see who did it," Lydia said. "Everyone hated Cameron, so it could be anyone."

"I like all the food metaphors," Patty said. "That's what makes a person hungry."

Jim nodded. "She has a food truck. What would that be like?"

"Hot?" Lydia suggested. "I bet everyone working in a food truck sweats all the time."

"Not if they have an air conditioner," Roberta said.

Jessa shook her head. "They can't leave the engine running all the time. I bet it's hot."

We got off topic so easily.

"Why isn't Murphy dressed up today?" Patty asked.

I shrugged. "I was too busy to deal with dress up."

Troy came in quietly and took an empty chair.

"Hey, Sheriff," Patty said. "We were just discussing whether a food truck would be a sweaty job."

"It seems like it would be. They probably have fans or something."

"So Jessica has a food truck, and she's in a famous baking show," Jim said. "There's a murder and Jessica looks guilty, so she has to solve the murder."

"Her aunt was annoying," Lydia said, "but I think all books need an annoying character."

"At least one," Patty agreed. "I need a character that isn't necessarily bad, but one that I can hate and not feel bad about."

"Exactly," Lydia said. "Like the snooty woman in *Emma* who marries Mr. Collins. I love to hate her, but she adds to the book."

Billie sighed. "We aren't talking about that book. Back to Jessica. Her biggest rival is killed, so obviously people are going to point at her."

"Billie thinks Jessica is like Jackie," Patty told Troy.

Troy sighed. "If you want me to tell you about Jackie, I'm off duty—and not in the mood."

Jim raised his eyebrows. "The sheriff is in a bad mood? I've never seen that before."

Troy smiled. "I'm not saying I'm in a bad mood. I just don't want to talk about any cases right now."

"Maybe the sheriff should go to Kellie's book club," Billie said. "They read romance. Then you wouldn't have to think about crime when you read."

Troy chuckled. "I'm not reading romance, and I'm not doing anything near Kellie if I don't have to."

"I like romance," Billie said. "I'm in both clubs. The last book we read keeps coming to my mind. The woman keeps getting carried by the man while she rests her head on his shoulder. It makes me wonder if that's really possible. If your arm is around a man's neck, how do you put your head on his shoulder? It seems too awkward."

Everyone stared at Billie for a moment, and then Roberta and Lydia began laughing. I thought of the one time Troy had carried me and I'd tried to put my head on his shoulder. It had been awkward. My arm and shoulder had gotten in the way. I wasn't going to bring that up.

"I think it would work," Jessa said, leaning her elbows on the table.

Lydia shook her head. "The person being carried would have to put their arm under the other person's arm and hold on to their shoulder to make it work, and then it might seem more like being carried like a baby."

"I'm not sure being carried is as romantic as we want it to be," Lydia said. "Every time my husband picks me up, I feel like I'm going to fall."

Lydia's husband was five foot four and probably a hundred and fifteen pounds. I wasn't sure that was a good example.

"Sheriff, pick someone up so we can see how well it works," Billie commanded.

Troy grinned. "I'm not sure that's what book club is about."

"Just do it," Patty encouraged, and then pointed at me. "Neeley's up for things. Pick her up."

I shook my head. That wasn't what I needed right now. "It won't work. My arm would get in the way."

"I need to see it to know for sure," Billie said. "It's not like we can do it in the other book club. Kellie's bossy and we have to stick to the subject she wants to talk about."

Troy stood and winked at me. "Come on, Neeley. Let's put Billie's question to rest."

"Fine," I mumbled, getting to my feet. Troy scooped me up, and I put my arm around his neck.

"Good, good," Billie said. "Now try to rest your head on his shoulder."

I leaned my head awkwardly, and it ended up on my own shoulder.

"Ha! I knew it wouldn't be practical. Same thing with kissing. Is it really any good to kiss in that position?"

"We aren't going there," I said, squirming to be put down.

"It would have to be annoying for the man, because he's holding up all that weight. How is he supposed to enjoy that?"

"What do you mean, all that weight?" I asked, glaring playfully at Billie.

She waved her hand in dismissal. "You know what I mean. Just try it. It's not like it counts as a real kiss. It's an experiment."

Troy grinned and sat me in my chair. "I think we'll have to go back to that one a different time. Are we going to talk about the book?"

"Right," Lydia said. "So, Jessica is a suspect and has to prove she's innocent."

Billie nodded. "Like Jackie."

Lydia rolled her eyes. "Except Jackie is guilty."

"How would you feel if everyone thought you were guilty and you weren't? Can you imagine what it would be like to have people think you were a killer?"

Roberta looked at me. "Neeley can tell us what that feels like."

"What do you mean?" Billie asked.

I shot Roberta a look, and she shrugged and mouthed, "Sorry."

"Neeley isn't a suspect," Troy said. "I don't want to go into everything, but there were multiple things at the diner."

"But the flowers that killed him were in Neeley's garden," Roberta said.

Patty's brows touched. "I thought a car hit him?"

Troy nodded. "It did. But there was something in his system that I'm told would have killed him anyway. The people who ran all the tests said he would have been dead in a few hours even if the car hadn't hit him."

Patty frowned. "I guess I'm not in on all the gossip these days."

"The flowers in Neeley's garden have to mean something," Roberta said. "How did they get there? And who would want to set her up?"

Troy grabbed a scone. "I'm not terribly concerned with that aspect of the case right now. I doubt someone came to Neeley's in advance to plant flowers so they could eventually kill Forrest. That's a long, strange plan. There are plenty of places a person could plant something around here and no one would know."

"Then where did the flowers come from?"

"Come on, Roberta," I teased. "Are you trying to make me look guilty?"

"No, I'm just curious."

"Well," Troy said, rubbing his chin, "It's possible the seeds blew over there and grew naturally."

"And just happen to be something similar to what Neeley planted?"

He shrugged. "I don't know enough about plants."

"I've been thinking," I said. "Sometimes people get moonflowers confused with datura. Maybe someone at the seed company I got them from got them confused as well. I've had that happen with other seeds before. They might have been mixed in with the moonflower seeds."

"That's true," Billie said. "I bought cucumber seeds one year and pumpkins grew."

"Does anyone else in town have datura plants growing?" Jessa asked.

Troy shrugged. "It would take a long time to check."

"But wouldn't it be worth the time to clear Neeley's name?"

Troy chuckled. "Come on, you guys. I told you. Neeley's not a suspect. There's plenty against Jackie to not make me worry about anyone else at the moment."

Roberta narrowed her eyes. "But what if it wasn't her? Then would you look around town for more datura flowers?"

"Yes, I would."

"We could do it," Jim offered. "It's not like most of us are busy. I walk around town every day. I could keep an eye out if someone tells me what they look like."

"So could I!" Patty said.

"I suppose I could," Billie said. "We don't want the wrong person going to prison, and the next most suspicious-looking person is Neeley."

Troy smiled at me, and I shook my head.

"I'm glad you're all trying to protect me," I said, "but I don't think it's an issue."

"That's what they all say until they're behind bars."

My mouth twitched. "Alright, if you all want to look around, I appreciate it."

Lydia tapped her lips. "I'll look at some of the houses on the outside of town. I can drive around." Most of our group couldn't drive.

"Let's start now," Billie said. "We can talk about the book in a few days. I like talking about them better when we've all read the entire thing, so we don't have to try and not give anything away."

Everyone got up and left. I remained seated, watching, and Troy's smile followed them.

"You have a loyal group here," he said.

"I do. Even if they are a bit paranoid."

"They do all read at least one mystery book a week. That might get you thinking differently."

"Did you read the book?"

"Yep."

"I'm surprised you keep reading them when you don't like the genre."

"It's growing on me. Besides, I have ulterior motives."

"Yeah?"

"One, I'm not going to tell you. The other is that I have a pathetic social life that consists of having dinner with my friend, his wife, and an old security guard."

A grin spread across my face. He'd told me that before. "And to expand your social circle, you come to Clover Haven for book club? You're really a party animal."

"I know. Any more excitement and I might have to retire."

I stood and stretched. "That's what book club is for. All the excitement."

"Murphy thinks so." Troy pointed to the corner. Murphy was sleeping on his back with his paws in the air.

"That dog can sleep in any position. It's almost impressive. So... are you going to tell me what you have on Jackie beside the flower petals?"

"Hmm. Probably not."

I punched him lightly on the arm. "Come on. Don't make me go snooping."

He smiled and shook his head. "You really need to meet Chase's wife. You would be best friends."

"Why is that? I've never done well with friends my age."

"She's always into something. She's solved a bunch of mysteries in Crystal Rock because she won't listen when I tell her to leave it to me."

"And her name is Harmony?"

"Yes."

"I can't imagine Chase married." I shook my head. "Stop changing the subject. What do you have on Jackie?"

He leaned against the wall and crossed his arms. "Well, I got a warrant so I could search everything. Her house, and car. That kind of thing. Also, her business records."

I sat on the table. "And?"

"Jackie's been telling people she doesn't care if the winery comes to town or not."

"Yeah, she told me. She said she doesn't make a lot on selling alcohol."

"That's a lie. I looked over her profit margins, she's barely scraping by most months. She takes in about one to five thousand a night on alcohol alone. Weekends are higher."

"Wow. I didn't think it would be anywhere near that."

"She is the only place in town people can sit and drink. She has some regulars. Most calls I get from Clover Haven for drunken brawls are Friday and Saturday nights and are at the diner."

"Are you serious? I guess I don't get out a lot. I didn't know we had a problem."

"Every place does, but it makes Jackie's claims void. Without that money, she would be out of business. There aren't enough people around to make a diner profitable."

"Interesting."

Troy sighed, rubbing a hand down his face. "I'd better go. I'm getting behind on paperwork."

"Aren't you off duty?"

"Yes, but that doesn't make it go away."

I walked him through the morgue and to the front doors. "Why aren't you going to tell me your first ulterior motive for coming to book club?"

He grinned. "Because it's the same reason I took a cake decorating class in high school."

I tilted my head. "Because you like to cook?"

"I hate to cook."

My eyes narrowed. "Then what is it?"

He opened the door but hesitated before stepping out. His voice dropped just a little. "I'm not sure you're ready to know."

Troy looked at me for a moment too long, like he was trying to decide if he should say more. Then he gave me the kind of smile that made my knees a little unsteady and walked into the night, leaving my heart racing and a thousand questions spinning in my head.

Chapter 11

"You want a tulip. On a boutonniere." I stared at the teenage girl in front of me.

"Yes." She pulled on her brown braid and looked at her two friends. They both nodded.

"Can I ask why?"

"I love tulips."

"Tulips are pretty, but they're not hardy. I doubt it can withstand a night of dancing. It will probably look bad for the entire day of the dance, and the petals will fall off. It will be a mess."

I would do it if they insisted, but not without letting them know it would be a disaster.

"There's nothing to make it last?"

"I suppose if you are really careful. That would mean no one touching it."

One of her friends giggled. "That would mean you couldn't dance close."

"That's very true," I affirmed. "The only way I can see it working is if I use a fake flower."

"Hmm. Can I look through the book again?"

"Sure."

I handed them an order book, and they went to the corner of the shop to look it over. There was a small round table with four chairs that people could use. They rarely got any use, because most people knew what they wanted when they came. Teenagers were always different.

If there were a dance next week, we would be busy. We'd already gotten several phone orders, and it wasn't even ten.

I tapped my fingers against the counter and stared blankly out the window. I hoped today stayed busy. I didn't need any extra time to wonder about what Troy had meant last night. I'd signed up for a cake decorating class in high school and had asked Troy and Chase to join me. Chase flat-out refused, but Troy had been excited.

If anyone else had told me they had had the same experience, I would have told them Troy liked them, but there was no way. Especially not in high school. Troy didn't get awkward or embarrassed. He thought everything was funny, even if it made him look bad. If he liked me, he would have told me.

"Yeah, she poisoned someone," one of the girls' voices carried to me. I glanced over and they all looked away and put their heads together.

"Should we be here, then?" one of them said.

I rolled my eyes. This shop was not big enough to whisper in.

"There's nowhere else to get flowers."

"I thought they arrested someone?"

"Yeah, but my mom said they got it wrong. It's a coverup."

I studied the girls. None of them looked familiar. If they were from a different town, then rumors were going far. Maybe I should be more worried about the datura than I was. Troy wasn't spreading rumors, so who could have told about the flowers?

"I'll be in the back," I told them. "Ring the bell when you're ready."

Roberta and Jessa were making wreaths. My online shop had caught on, and we had been selling seasonal wreaths almost every day. It took time, but I wasn't going to complain. I tried to get my shop to pay for itself. I have the money my parents left me, but I preferred to come out ahead.

"Does this pass as Halloween and fall?" Roberta asked, holding up a wreath of orange leaves and pumpkins.

"Probably?" I wanted to tell her something less orange might help, but I didn't want to hurt her feelings. The small pumpkins were hard to see against the orange leaves.

"I'm thinking of sticking some small bats on it."

Jessa smiled and shook her head.

Roberta put the wreath on the table. "Are there still people in the front?"

"Yes. Three girls getting ready for prom. They keep asking for odd things like tulips."

Jessa raised her brow. "That would be a mess. Do you want me to go out there and tell them what they want?"

I laughed. "If you want."

She stood and straightened her flowery blouse. "I love telling people what they want."

I sat to work on a wreath as she left.

"Maybe you should stop asking kids what they want for flowers. Just have one kind, and only let them pick the color."

"I think they like to choose. Of course, there are always some who seem clueless."

Murphy came over and sniffed a flower, then wandered into the front. The girls out there all began talking to him and telling him how cute he was. I smiled. Most people couldn't resist his mushy, adorable face.

"Roses are always classy," Jessa told the girls. "You can never go wrong with a rose. Anything else could be a mistake."

"Then I guess I'll use a rose," one girl said. "What color do you think is best?"

"What color is your date's tie?"

"Blue."

"Then I would go with white."

"Great. I'll do that."

I turned to Roberta. "How does she do that? No one ever cares about my opinion, and I know more than anyone around here about flowers."

Roberta laughed. "I listen to you."

Murphy ran in and barked at the wall.

"What's the problem, Murph?"

He put his front paws on the wall and kept barking.

"I'll get him," Roberta said, standing. "I need a break." She picked Murphy up, and he tried to get down. "What's wrong, boy?"

He barked again.

Jessa came back and flexed her arm. "Jessa saves the day again."

"Thanks," I told her. "I can never get teenagers to decide."

The bell above the shop rang, and Murphy jumped to the floor. I went out to see one of the girls who had just left. Murphy was at my heels.

"Is there a problem?"

She pointed to her right. "Someone made a big mess with your flowers out there. It wasn't like that when we came."

"Alright, thanks."

I went outside with Murphy and around the side of the shop. "What?" All the flowers that had been planted there had been torn out and thrown all over the grass. I stepped around them, looking for any datura flowers.

Murphy pushed his nose through the torn flowers.

"Careful, Murph."

"Oh my," Jessa said, coming over. "Someone did this while we were inside! How did we miss it?"

"Tearing up flowers wouldn't make much sound. I bet that's why Murphy was barking at the wall. He must have heard something."

Roberta rounded the corner and paused. "Good gravy. Who would do this?"

"I'm not sure, but it wasn't Jackie. I'm trying to find any of the datura plants, but I'm not seeing any."

Jessa kicked some of the plants. "Does that mean the sheriff arrested the wrong person?"

I shook my head. "I don't know. Or maybe more than one person is involved. Or... maybe someone wants Jackie to look innocent."

Murphy ran over to me with something in his mouth. "Can I have that?" I asked him, taking it out of his mouth.

"What is it?" Roberta asked. "A credit card?"

"No," I said, turning it over. "It's a name tag from the store." I stared down at Pedro's name. I turned it to show them.

"What? No," Roberta said, "Pedro wouldn't do this, and he wouldn't kill anyone."

"I'm not saying anything," I said. "I'm just showing you what it is."

"That looks pretty obvious to me," Jessa said.

I nodded. "But, is it too obvious?"

"Yes!" Roberta said, pointing at it. "Way too obvious. Someone planted it."

"But we can't just assume that," Jessa told her. "He could have been tearing everything up and lost it."

"But we also can't assume it was him."

"Who would want to frame him?"

I shrugged. "Who would want to frame anyone? I feel like this is still aimed at me. They could be hoping I'll look guilty by destroying the evidence."

"Shouldn't we call the police?" Jessa said.

"I'll call Troy." I took out my phone and dialed him, but I went to voicemail. "Hey, Troy. Someone tore up a bunch of my flowers outside the shop. All the datura is gone. Bye." I hated leaving messages. I found it hard to know how much to say.

"What's the plan?" Roberta asked.

"I need to look around the grocery store, but I've looked at the locks on the doors and I can't pop those."

"We could go take Pedro his name tag and see how guilty he looks," Jessa said.

Roberta put a hand on her ample hip and glared. "Except he won't look guilty, just confused, because he didn't do it."

Jessa held up her hands in surrender. "Calm down. I'm just keeping an open mind."

A car drove down the road toward the shop.

"That's Vivian's car," Jessa said. "She must be back."

Vivian parked and walked over to us, her eyes scanning the mess.

"How are you, Vivian?" Jessa asked, giving her a quick squeeze.

She shrugged. "Some days are better than others."

"Did you just get back?"

"Last night."

"Is there anything we can help you with?" I asked.

"Flowers. Lots of flowers. We put off Forrest's funeral because of all the stuff surrounding his death, but now I need to get planning." She dabbed at her eyes. "I don't know where to start."

"Don't worry. We can help you. What is your price range?"

She rubbed her nose. "Anything. I want it to be nice. It's hard to care about money now that Forrest is gone. I feel ridiculous. I spent so much time worried about losing money, and now I've realized that without Forrest, nothing matters. I wanted money to travel with him and make a life. Now money is just... hollow."

Jessa patted her shoulder. "Why don't you come in and we can help you?"

She nodded, then turned to me. "My gardener is great. I know you like to be independent, but I think you might need some expert help out here." She gestured at the mess.

"I didn't do this," I said. "We just came out, and it was like this." I tucked Pedro's name tag into my pocket. No one needed to know about that yet.

"That's odd. Still, if you want the name of my gardener, let me know."

"Thanks."

We went inside and I got Murphy comfy in the back room. When I went to the front, Jessa was showing Vivian some of her options in a book.

"Will you stay in town?" I asked her.

Her mouth turned down. "I'm not sure. I love my house, but the town isn't my favorite. I could sell it. I know Mr. Valenzuela would buy it in a heartbeat."

I cocked my head. "Pedro?"

"Yes."

"He wants your house?"

"Yes. I guess he grew up in that house."

I frowned. "I don't remember that."

"That's because you weren't born," Roberta said. "Or you were young at the time. His parents sold it when he was a teenager."

"He's approached us several times, offering to buy it," Vivian said. "He even offered more than market value."

"He must be sentimental."

Roberta nodded. "He is. Pedro was so mad when his parents sold it. He moved out on his own soon after."

Maybe Forrest's death hadn't been because of the winery. Maybe it had been about selling the house. Still, Roberta was right. Pedro didn't seem like the violent type. Not that people couldn't surprise you.

I was going to have to get into the store, and then if I didn't find anything, I would search his house. We couldn't have the wrong person going to jail.

Chapter 12

"This is crazy," Roberta whispered. We were crouched down behind a cardboard display of a new cereal in Pedro's store. "Someone is going to see us."

"Shh! If we aren't quiet, they'll find us for sure." I peeked around the corner. The store was small, with only a few aisles. We were planning to stay here until it closed and everyone was gone. That would be another ten minutes, then however long it took for the two employees to lock up and leave.

"Are you sure they clean in the morning?" I whispered.

Roberta nodded. "Someone comes in at five."

My leg was getting a cramp, and Roberta shifted her position every minute or so. We should have waited longer to hide, but we didn't want anyone to be watching for us to leave. By now, everyone should have forgotten we had been here.

When the lights flipped off, I sighed with relief and stood, stretching my legs.

"Oh, man," Roberta said. "You're gonna have to pull me up."

I held out my hands and helped her to her feet.

"Let's wait to come out for a minute," I said under my breath.

Roberta rolled her ankles. "So long as we aren't squatting. I'm going to be sore for days."

As soon as we were sure we were alone, we crept around the display.

"There's only one camera," I said, pointing over near the checkout. "I think it only focuses near the doors."

Roberta nodded. "What are we looking for?"

"Anything suspicious."

"In the food?"

"No. If there's any evidence, my guess is that it's in Pedro's office."

We went to the back of the store and into a small, dark hallway. We passed the restrooms and maintenance closet and tried the knob on Pedro's office.

"Unlocked!" I said, pushing it open.

"That's convenient," Roberta said, entering.

I cringed. "I forgot to bring gloves." I flipped the light on with my elbow.

"Oh boy," Roberta said. "It looks like Pedro is a slob."

I smiled. Roberta wasn't much better. Her house scared me.

Papers weren't only scattered all over the computer desk, but they were crumpled and surrounding the garbage can.

"I'm not sure how to proceed," I admitted. "Without being able to touch anything, we can't look in drawers."

"There are enough papers around, I guess we can see what they say." Roberta went to the desk and her eyes scanned the documents.

I inspected the garbage and moved some things around with my foot, but I couldn't see anything helpful.

"How does he run this place with this mess?" Roberta mumbled. "I hope he has good records online."

Lights from a car shone in the window, and we dropped to the ground.

"That's Pedro's parking spot!" Roberta said, her voice in a panic.

"Great," I muttered. "Crawl out of here."

"Should we turn off the light?"

"No. Whoever's out there would have seen the light was on. It would be more suspicious to turn it off."

We crawled on the hard, flat carpet until we got into the hall. As soon as we were out of shot of the window, we stood and ran into the store area. We went back behind the display, but this time, we sat on the floor. If Pedro was coming this late, it was probably to do office work, not be out here.

The steps in the back hallway seemed exaggeratedly slow and loud. Roberta was breathing so loudly that someone might hear us if they came out here.

I closed my eyes and heard a few doors open and close. I wondered if Pedro paid security officers to come check things at night.

"Hello?" Pedro's voice carried across the store. "I know you're in here. Come out."

I swallowed hard and looked at Roberta's dark shadow.

"He's bluffing," I whispered.

"I'm going to call the police in one... two..."

"Get out," Roberta whispered. "I've got this." She stood, and before I could stop her, she stepped out into the dark. "I'm here."

"Roberta?" Pedro said with disbelief in his voice. "Is that you?"

"Yes."

The lights turned on, and I squinted in the brightness.

Roberta moved away from where I was, and my mind ran in circles trying to figure out a way out of this.

"What are you doing here?" he asked. "I didn't expect you to rob me."

"Rob you?" Roberta asked. "Why would I rob you?"

"What are you doing?"

Roberta sighed. "We've been friends forever, right?"

"Right."

"Does that mean I can give you some honest, constructive criticism?"

I peeked through a crack in the display and saw Pedro running a hand through his black hair. "I suppose so," he said.

"I love this chocolate milk," she said, grabbing a single-serving container from the refrigerated section. I wanted to slap my forehead.

"Okay...?" Pedro looked baffled. If I weren't hiding behind this cardboard stand eavesdropping, I would have smiled.

"This one expires in three days," Roberta said, holding it in front of her. She pulled another one out from the back. "This one in the back expires in ten days. You put the older ones in the front. I want the freshest one."

Pedro blinked twice. "Um—"

"You should put the fresh ones in the front. I don't want you to lose customers, so I was rearranging your milk for you."

There was no way he was going to buy that.

"Roberta... all the milk is fresh. If it expires, I get rid of it. If you taste one from the front and one from the back, one isn't going to taste different from the other."

"I don't know about that."

"Look, if I put all the newer milk in the front, people will buy that, and the other stuff will expire. I can't run a store like that, I'd lose money."

Roberta put the milk back. "I guess that makes sense. Sorry. I thought I was helping."

"It's fine, but please don't come in here after hours. How did you get in here?"

"I was here late, and the lights went off."

"I'll have to talk to the guy who closed up."

Great. Now we'd probably gotten someone in trouble.

"Don't blame him," Roberta said. "I kind of avoided him."

"Ah, I see."

"Sorry. I'm very passionate about my chocolate milk."

He chuckled. "I see that."

"Too bad you sell it for the same price as a gallon of milk in the city."

He shrugged. "It's what I have to do to stay in business." He walked over to the chocolate milk and took one down. "Here. You can have this one."

"Thanks!" Roberta said, taking the bottle.

"Let me walk you out. And next time you have a problem with the way I do something, come tell me, okay?"

"Okay. Sorry again."

While they walked and talked, I took advantage of the distraction and ran to the back hallway, slipping out the back door before anyone could notice. Roberta wouldn't be expecting to meet up again, so I started the trek home through the dark.

That had been close—and worse, we hadn't figured anything out.

⚜

"Morning," Troy said, entering the flower shop.

I smiled from behind the counter. "Morning."

He walked around the shop, looking at the flower arrangements decorating the place. My smile fell as I watched him. He wasn't usually a flower admirer. Was he looking for clues?

"You never called me back," I told him.

He walked casually over to the counter and rested his arms on top. "What are you talking about?"

"I left you a message? About the mess outside?"

His mouth turned down. "I saw that out there, but I didn't get a message."

"Someone ripped out all the flowers on that side—and the datura flowers are gone."

"Can I go look?"

"Yep. I'll take you." I looked in the back at Roberta and Jessa. "I'll be outside for a minute."

Troy and I went to assess the damage. "When did this happen?"

"Yesterday at about ten."

"You were inside?"

"Yes. We had some teenagers come in to order flowers, and when they left, they noticed it."

"Could they have done it?"

"No. They wouldn't have had time."

"Murphy found this in the mess." I pulled out Pedro's badge, and he took it.

"That explains one thing."

"What?"

Troy's lips twitched. "Pedro told me about finding Roberta in his store last night. It all sounded very... peculiar, but also very Roberta. I'm guessing she wasn't alone."

I tried to look confused.

He smiled. "Don't give me that look, Neeley. You were in the store trying to figure out why Pedro's badge was in there."

"What are you talking about?"

"You know, Pedro has cameras that detect movement? I'm sure he captured you doing something."

I deflated. "Okay fine. I was there."

His eyes sparkled. "I thought so."

"Do you think Pedro will look at the video?"

His smile grew. "The cameras are just for show. They don't actually record."

I slammed my shoulder into him, and he laughed.

"You're such a punk," I said. "And a liar."

"I don't have time to wait around for you to confess."

"What do you think about this?" I asked, motioning to the mess of flowers.

He squatted down and picked up a moonflower. "I'm not sure. I wonder if one of Jackie's friends is trying to get off the hook. If they did this, they might think everyone would assume she was innocent since she couldn't have done it."

"Have you been telling people about the flowers?" I asked. "I overheard some girls talking about me yesterday. They sounded convinced I'd killed Forrest."

"I haven't, but you know how it is around here. If one person knows, everyone knows."

"Do you think Pedro might have done this?"

"I'm not sure. If he didn't, someone is definitely trying to frame him."

I looked up at him. "Did you know Pedro wanted to buy Forrest's house?"

"No."

"That's the house he grew up in. He offered more than it was worth, Vivian told me."

"Interesting. It's a nice house, but nothing out of the ordinary."

"Pedro wouldn't kill Forrest to get the house, would he?"

"I doubt Pedro would kill someone for any reason."

"I think Roberta has a crush on him."

Troy smiled. "I could see them together."

"They've known each other their entire life. If nothing's happened in fifty-five or so years, it never will."

"Don't give up on it completely. Maybe they just need a little nudge."

I shook my head. "Maybe after we find out whether or not he's a killer."

Chapter 13

"What's the gossip about you being a murderer?" Grandpa asked me at dinner.

I dropped my fork. "That's all it is. A rumor."

"You know Forrest Cutler's body arrived today?"

I took a drink. "It's in the basement?"

"Yes. I guess the police are done with whatever it is they do. I talked to some folks in town, they said there was something going around about you."

"Forrest had datura in him. I'm sure you already know that?"

He nodded and scratched his fingers through his gray hair. "I do."

"Somehow, datura was mixed in with my moonflowers that are growing around the shop. The police aren't investigating me, but some people like to talk about anything."

"What does the sheriff think?"

"Since when do you care what Troy thinks?" My grandpa had never pretended to like Troy.

"I just want to know what to expect."

"He knows it wasn't me."

"Are you sure?"

"Positive. What would my motive be? I had nothing to gain in Forrest's death."

"But since you dated—"

"Why does everyone keep saying that? One date. It was nothing, and it was like eighteen years ago. I never liked Forrest."

"Then why did you date him?"

"On my heck, Grandpa. One date is not dating."

"Why did he only ask you once? I'm starting to wonder why you don't date more. You're a beautiful girl with lots of talents."

I wasn't sure whether to be flattered or offended. My grandpa rarely complimented me.

"I don't want to date."

"Why?"

I sighed and leaned back. "Because the only person I want to date doesn't want to date me."

"Are we talking about Troy? I thought you were over him."

"I am. I was."

"And then he came back." It wasn't a question. "Well, he's an idiot."

"He is not."

"He is, or he would want to date you."

"Grandpa," I groaned. "Just leave it."

"Have you actually ever asked him if he wants to date you?"

"Of course not."

"Then how do you know he doesn't?"

"Troy isn't the kind of person who's scared to do things like that. If he ever liked me, he would have told me." I fiddled with my fork.

"How many girls did he date in high school?"

"Pretty much all of them."

"But how many were his actual girlfriend?"

"None."

"He's scared. He likes you."

"Grandpa, you are crazy."

He laughed. "I can't disagree with that. Why don't you have him over for dinner? I'll have a little talk with him."

My eyes went wide. "Absolutely not! You aren't allowed to ever tell him anything about it, or anyone else, for that matter. If you do, I'll know it was you, because no one else knows."

"Fine, fine. I need to go to bed. Will you check the lights and locks before you turn in?"

"Sure. Do you want dessert?"

He stood and stabilized himself with the table. "No. The doctor told me my knees aren't ever going to get better if I don't lose a lot of weight. Oh, did I tell you someone broke in earlier?"

"No! Did you call the police?"

"Of course. The sheriff came and looked around."

"What did he say?"

"I don't know. I didn't talk to him after he was here. Goodnight."

It was just like Grandpa to dump something like that on me and act like it was no big deal. He either over-reacted or under-reacted. It was anyone's guess which.

I cleaned up and went around checking all the locks and lights. When I opened the basement door, I sighed. The light was on. The basement held the dead bodies and wasn't the place I liked to go at night.

Whoever built this place hadn't planned for it to be a morgue. That came later. The light switch was all the way at the bottom of the stairs. When I was little and had to turn off the lights, I'd run as fast as I could. If Troy or Chase were around, I made them come with me. Grandpa had finally gotten into the habit of switching the lights off when he was done, but he still forgot every now and then.

I took a deep breath and walked down the stairs at a steady pace, reminding myself I was a grown woman and didn't need to be scared of a dark basement filled with dead bodies. When I reached the bottom, I braced myself to flip the light switch—then run back up.

"Wait!" someone called.

I screamed and spun around to see Troy standing next to the refrigerated body drawers.

He laughed, and I stomped over to him, arms crossed.

"What are you doing in here?" I snapped. "You almost gave me a heart attack!"

"Walt called me." He smiled and hugged me. "You're shaking. I guess growing up doesn't make turning the lights off any less scary?"

"I would've been fine if you hadn't been lurking down here. My grandpa made it sound like you were gone." I pulled away. "Did you find anything?"

"Yes. Someone got in through a window."

"Did they take anything?"

"Not that I can tell, but I don't know what's supposed to be here. Maybe you can look around and check?"

I wandered the room, scanning the shelves and drawers. "Nothing looks like it's missing."

He held up a bright purple button in his gloved hand. "I found this."

"It's not Grandpa's. He only wears a few colors, and purple isn't one of them."

"Has anyone else come down here today?"

"No. Not today."

"Remember when we used to dare each other to look in the coolers?"

I smiled slightly. "We were odd kids. And now you probably look in them all the time."

"More than I want to, that's for sure."

"Where was the button?"

"On the floor over here." He walked to a spot and pointed. "How well does it get cleaned down here? It might've been here a while."

"It gets swept daily." I squinted at him. "Why do you have glitter all over your backside?"

Troy twisted, trying to look behind himself. "I don't know. Why are you looking?"

I rolled my eyes. "You're such a dork."

He laughed. "It's on my gloves too. Let me pull Forrest out again and take another look. I leaned against the shelf when I opened the cooler. That's when I saw the button. There was some glitter, but I couldn't figure out where it'd come from."

He grabbed one of the handles on the body drawer and pulled. I wrinkled my nose. I'd been around bodies my entire life, but I didn't like to see them, especially when they were getting older.

A sheet shielded the body from sight, but gold glitter covered one side of the shelf.

"Why would there be glitter?" I asked, inspecting it.

Troy shrugged. "No idea. I figured it must be some weird family thing or something."

"Weird family thing?"

"You never know what people are going to do. I was at a funeral once where the family poured pennies all over a guy."

"They clean the body, though, so if it was a family thing, some of the family would have had to come in. I'll ask Grandpa tomorrow."

"Is he in bed?"

"Yeah, and you don't want to mess with him after he goes to bed."

"I seem to remember that."

"So, all you have to go by is the button and glitter?"

"That's what it looks like." He ran a hand through his hair. "I think I need to set Jackie free. There are too many things that make it look like it might have been someone else."

"Unless there is more than one thing going on. Or she had an accomplice."

"Both are possible, but I'm not sure I can hold her with everything that's happening. I might need to let her go and tell her she has to stay in town."

"She never confessed?"

"No, and she said she'd never seen the canister in her kitchen, or the dried flowers. She claims someone planted them to frame her."

"What do you think?"

"I'm not sure."

"Shouldn't you have a deputy with you? You do everything alone."

"We're stretched too thin. It would be ideal, but sometimes it doesn't happen."

"Isn't that dangerous?" I folded my arms across my body. I didn't enjoy imagining Troy in danger, and that's how he spent every day.

"It can be." He pushed the drawer shut.

"For some reason, I thought sheriffs were more like mascots. I thought they did all the media stuff."

"That might happen in some places, but not in small towns."

I pointed at the stairs. "I'm going up. Are you coming?"

"I guess I'm done."

"Turn off the light." I hurried up the steps.

"Chicken."

I laughed and went through the door. Troy was close behind.

"You should have Walt move the light switch to the top of the stairs," he said.

I grinned. "Then I would have turned the lights off and you would have been all by yourself with a bunch of dead guys in the dark."

"Yeah, but I'm not a chicken."

"Hmm. You were quick to tell me not to turn it off when you were down there."

He smiled. "Yeah, but that was because I would have had to move around in the pitch dark to turn it back on, and you would have yelled a lot louder if you'd switched it off and then I'd told you I was there."

"That's probably true."

He yawned. "It's been a long day."

"It's late and you still have to drive home."

"I'm getting used to it. I've spent more time in Clover Haven in the last month than I have in the last five years."

"I bet Grandpa would let you have a room here. Then you could stay when you were just going to be back the next day."

He chuckled. "You think Walt would let me stay? Maybe in one of the body freezers."

I gave him my best smile. "Do you want me to ask him? About the room, not the body freezer."

"I suppose. I guess stranger things have happened."

Chapter 14

We were discussing a paranormal mystery today, and that meant I was in my witch dress. I'd paid enough for it; I figured I better wear it a few more times, and it didn't hurt that Troy had seemed impressed last time.

"You're looking good," I told Murphy. He had a sorcerer's hat on his head. He kept trying to bite it off, but so far hadn't been able to. "Come on. Let's go. We have time to talk to Grandpa before people arrive."

I found him watching a movie. Murphy ran to the couch and jumped up, cuddling next to Grandpa.

"Don't get too comfy, Murph. It's book club tonight."

"Book club?" Grandpa asked. "What's with the outfit?"

"We dress up according to the book we read."

"Like cosplay?"

I shrugged.

"Aren't you all a little old for that?" he grumbled.

I smiled. "Well, I'm the youngest of the group, so I'm alright with it."

"Does Jim dress up?"

"Sometimes."

"Maybe I should come for entertainment."

"You're welcome to. Can I ask a favor?"

He raised his brow. "I suppose."

"Troy keeps ending up in Clover Haven. It's a long drive going back and forth every day. Can he stay in one of the empty rooms when he's in town?"

He sighed. "Fine."

I blinked. "Really?"

"I'm getting old and soft."

"Thanks, Grandpa."

He nodded. I grabbed Murphy, and we went to the book club room. Patty was already there, putting tarts on the table.

"Hello," she said. "I love that dress."

"I love yours. Is it new?"

She smiled. "Yes. Every woman should get a new witch dress every now and again."

"That's the truth," Billie said, entering the room.

A smile broke across my face. A tall pink witch hat covered her short gray curls, and she wore a lacy pink dress and ballet shoes.

Jim and Lydia came in behind her. Jim was dressed like a vampire. That was new. Roberta and Jessa weren't far behind. Troy was last, and came in with a pack of soda.

"You didn't dress up," I said.

He smiled at me. "No, but I'm glad you did."

"Don't be a dork."

"You've called me a dork twice in the last twenty-four hours."

"It must be true then." I stuck my tongue out at him and immediately felt like a teenager again.

"I brought soda. Now I can say I've contributed."

Everyone found a seat, and Troy turned to everyone. "Does anyone in here own a bright purple shirt with buttons?"

Everyone looked confused and shook their heads.

Troy sat down. "Just wondering."

"The only person brave enough to wear something like that is Pedro," Roberta said. "He has the ugliest purple shirt. He wears it at least once a week."

Jim chuckled. "I've teased him about it before. I told him people can probably see him from space."

Troy nodded at me. I figured that meant he'd found out what he wanted, and it was time to change the subject.

"Okay, everyone. What did we think about *Double, Double, Hex and Trouble*? Remember, we're only doing this book for one week, so say what you want. Spoilers allowed."

"I hated it," Billie said.

Jim smiled. "Why, because you didn't guess who the murderer was?"

"No, I didn't. And do you know why?"

"Because they didn't even introduce the killer until the last chapter," Patty said.

"Yes," Billie nodded. "That's not fair. He should have been mentioned at least once earlier on."

"My problem was the love story," Roberta said. "I'm usually all for love triangles, but I didn't like either guy. Neither one of them had rippling muscles."

Troy snorted, and I smiled.

"Who cares about that?" Jessa said. "It's about their personality."

"Well, I need to be able to daydream, okay?"

"Who's going to read book two to see if she turns Henry back into a human?"

"Not me," Lydia said. "Henry's better off as a salamander. He can't talk that way."

"What about you, Neeley?" Billie asked. "What did you think?"

"I didn't have a strong opinion about it. I might read the second one if I have time."

"Sheriff? What about you?"

Troy gave a sheepish grin and shrugged. "There wasn't an audiobook, and I didn't get around to it. I opened it on my phone a few times, but I kept nodding off."

"That's what I'm saying," Billie said. "No more books by this author."

Murphy jumped up, trying to see what was happening. Patty picked him up, and he put his paws on the table. His tongue hung out, and he made weird snorting sounds.

"Murphy thinks we should read a dog book next," Jim said. "It's been a while."

"What did you think about this one?" Roberta asked him.

"I skimmed a big portion of it. It was hard to get into. I was a fan of Henry until he became a salamander."

"Really?" Jessa asked. "I thought it served him right."

"I heard Jackie is back home," Lydia said randomly.

Everyone turned to Troy.

"Yeah, I'm not sure we had enough evidence against her. I'm not saying she's innocent, but I think I need to see things more clearly, considering some recent events."

"Like someone tearing up Neeley's flowers?" Roberta asked. "We know she didn't do it, because we were with her when it happened. I mean, she probably looks guilty since she had the flowers growing there in the first place, but she had no reason to kill Forrest."

My smile was lopsided. Why did everyone have to keep bringing me into things?

"I heard Neeley was in Forrest's will," Patty said. "That's getting some people talking. We need to prove to everyone she's innocent."

"Whoa, whoa, whoa," I said. "I'm not in his will. We barely knew each other."

"I've been looking around for more datura flowers," Jim said. "I haven't seen any. Not that I'm an expert on flowers or anything."

"I haven't found any either," Lydia said. "I looked for hours."

"Thanks, you guys, but I'm not worried. Troy knows what he's doing, so I'm sure he'll arrest the right person."

"Well, he's already arrested the wrong person," Billie said.

"We don't know that."

"Jackie has been understanding," Troy said. "And like Neeley told you, we still don't know she's innocent. She still has the most stuff pointing at her, I'm just nervous about the fact that things that might be related have been happening while she was locked up."

"If it wasn't her, you might have to look into Neeley, just so people don't think you're protecting your friend," Roberta said.

"Are you serious?" I asked. "Do you think I did it?"

Roberta laughed. "Of course not. I just feel like there's a lot of stuff pointing at you, so he needs to address that so people don't talk."

"How do we always get so off topic?" Jessa asked.

"It's not off topic," Billie told her. "It's just our lives versus the characters in the book. It's all solving mysteries, so it's related."

"I suppose, but I think you all need to give Neeley and the sheriff a break. Neeley is innocent, and Sheriff McGregor is doing the best he can."

"Thanks, Jessa," Troy said.

The rest of the evening was more mellow. By the time everyone but Troy had left, I was ready to go to bed. Murphy had already fallen asleep on the floor.

I wasn't sure why Troy was taking so long to leave. He cleaned up the table and made small talk. Then I remembered Grandpa.

"My grandpa said you can have a room here."

"Really? That's surprising."

"He agreed immediately. I thought I was going to have to beg. You can use the room whenever you want. You can even change the lock if you want and leave spare clothes here."

"Thanks. That will be nice. A half hour isn't a terrible drive, but it's annoying sometimes."

"Do you want to stay tonight?"

"Sure. I need to be here in the morning to check a few things."

"Come on." I took him to a room and opened the door. "I didn't think. It's been a while since anyone's stayed here. It's probably all dusty. Even the bed."

"I don't care about stuff like that. It will be fine."

"I can get you fresh bedding."

He went to the bed and brushed his hand over it. "Don't worry about it."

"Do you have clean clothes? I could grab some of Grandpa's pajamas. They might fit two of you, though."

He smiled. "I keep a spare in my truck."

"I would let you use Aunt Gina's room again, but you never know when she might show up. With this one, you can come and go and not worry about anyone bothering anything."

"The only snoopy person around is you, so I'm not so sure about that," he teased.

I rolled my eyes, but a smile still came. "I'm not going to go through your things. At least not unless you become a suspect in something."

His lips twitched. "Good to know."

"Do you need anything?"

"Nope. Go to bed. You've looked ready for the last half hour."

"I am tired. I changed the oil in my car today, and it took longer than I expected."

"You changed it yourself?"

"Yep. Chase taught me a long time ago, remember?"

"Right. I should have had him teach me."

I gave him a tired smile. "You still don't know how to change your own oil?"

"No."

"I'll teach you sometime. Or you can pay me and I'll do it."

He grinned. "I bet you'd charge me more than the place I go."

"Double."

"I thought so."

"Let me know if you need anything. Goodnight."

"Night."

I went back to the other room to grab Murphy and carried him to his bed. Then I pulled on my pajamas and brushed my teeth. I'd had trouble sleeping the night before since so much was happening lately. I knew Troy thought I was innocent. Still, it bugged me knowing other people were talking about it.

Things needed to speed up. Now that Jackie was free, I could talk to her—and hopefully finally get some answers.

Chapter 15

"Sheriff's here," Roberta said, peering out the shop window. "He's got someone with him."

I looked up but kept watering the flowers arranged along the display. "Who is it?"

"Someone I don't know. He's wearing a suit."

I moved behind the counter. I was pretty sure Troy wasn't bringing me a customer, but being back there made me feel a little more prepared—just in case.

They entered, and I smiled politely. I'd never seen the man before. He looked to be around forty, with neatly combed dark hair and a sharp blue tie. His serious expression made me nervous.

"Hi, Neeley. Roberta," Troy said. "How are you today?"

"Great," I said. Troy was smiling, but it didn't reach his eyes. Something was wrong, and I wasn't sure I wanted to know what.

"This is Kevin Freeman," Troy continued. "Kevin, this is Neeley Kelter and Roberta Kinney. Kevin is Forrest Cutler's lawyer."

"Oh," I said, not sure how else to respond.

"Kevin needs to talk to you," Troy said, looking straight at me.

I took a deep breath. Why would Forrest's lawyer want to talk to me? No one had charged me with anything, so I couldn't imagine why I'd need a conversation with an attorney.

Roberta excused herself and slipped into the back.

I kept my nervous smile in place. "We can sit over here," I said, motioning to the small round table. The three of us sat, and I tried not to look as unsettled as I felt.

Mr. Freeman handed me an envelope with my name scrawled across the front in messy handwriting. "Sheriff McGregor said things are busy around here, so I'll get straight to the point. Forrest Cutler left you some money in his will."

My eyes widened. "What? That doesn't make any sense."

"He left you ten thousand dollars."

"Great," I muttered. "Forrest was crazy. I don't want it."

Troy nodded. "Told you she'd say that."

"He also left you that letter," Mr. Freeman added, motioning to the envelope in my hand.

"Should I read it out loud?" I asked, pulling out the paper.

"Up to you," he said. "I already know what it says."

"I'm dying to know," Troy said.

I cleared my throat. "'Dear Neeley, You're probably confused right now. But I want you to have this money. I think you deserve it, since I never would have passed calculus without you. I know you didn't want to cheat, but I appreciated the way you always placed your paper just right on your desk so I could see it. That was good of you.'"

I stared at the letter, then looked up. "He cheated off my papers? How did I not notice?"

Troy smirked. "Do you remember what you were like during tests? You were intense—and the only person I know who *liked* taking tests. You didn't notice anything but the paper in front of you."

He had a point. I'd always been a good test taker—and I enjoyed them. Probably not something I should brag about.

"What else does it say?" Troy asked.

I took a deep breath and kept reading. "'I always thought something might happen between us. I've often wondered what your silky hair would feel like, and your shining blue eyes pierce my soul. You were my dream for so long, but I guess no one could ever compare to—'" I stopped mid-sentence. Oh no. I was *not* reading that out loud. "Hold on." I skipped down a few lines. "'I finally moved on, but you've always been close to my heart. Take this money and go on a nice vacation. Yours always, Forrest.'"

"Wow," Troy said.

"Wow, nothing," I muttered. "If I'd known he was that crazy, I would have avoided him more than I did."

Troy leaned back in his chair. "What did that one sentence say that you skipped?"

"Don't worry about it."

Mr. Freeman coughed, clearly trying not to smile. *Great.* The lawyer knew exactly what Forrest had written.

I turned to him. "I don't want the money. What happens if I don't take it?"

"It would likely pass to Forrest's wife, Vivian."

"Good. That's who should have it. Does she know about this?"

"Yes."

"Even the letter?"

"Probably not. Forrest gave me all the sealed envelopes to deliver after his passing."

I blew air through my bangs and looked at Troy. "This doesn't make any sense. We talked sometimes, but aside from that one dance, I never thought anything of it."

Troy shrugged. "He was pretty quiet in high school. Maybe he didn't want you to know."

I glanced at Mr. Freeman. "Is there anything I need to do to officially say no?"

"You'll need to sign something stating you're declining the inheritance," Mr. Freeman said. "I can draw that up for you, or you can write it yourself."

"How long ago did Forrest write his will?" I asked, hoping the answer was *right after high school*. Anything else would feel... slimy.

"About three years ago."

I exhaled sharply. "Forrest had issues. I'm honestly glad I didn't know about all this when he was alive."

Mr. Freeman handed me a business card. "I have a few more stops to make. Call me if you need anything."

I nodded. He shook both our hands and left the shop.

Troy turned to me with a goofy grin. "You know I'm never going to sleep again until I find out what you didn't read out loud."

I shook my head and smirked. "Then I hope you enjoy insomnia, because you're not seeing it." I slid the paper back into the envelope and tucked it under my arm.

"Don't tell me Forrest knew who you had a crush on in high school and you never told me or Chase? We tried everything to get that out of you."

"And that's exactly why I never said anything. You two would have been unbearable."

"Probably. But now I *have* to know. Who would Forrest have guessed that even I didn't figure out?"

"Who says he was even right?"

"If he wasn't, you would've read it."

"Maybe." I offered an innocent smile.

He narrowed his eyes playfully. "I'll ask Chase. He might remember something."

I pointed the envelope at him. "You better not. I don't need you and Chase dissecting my high school feelings."

"Let me read the letter, and I won't say a word. I won't even tease you."

My heart skipped. If he saw his name written in that space... "No way."

He leaned in with mock suspicion. "It wasn't *Chase*, was it? That would've made things real awkward back then."

I laughed. "Definitely not. I already told you I didn't see him that way. Now stop guessing. I've got work to do."

Troy let out a dramatic sigh. "Fine. I guess I should get back to mine." He stood and stretched.

My smile faded. "Do you think this is going to cause trouble for me?"

"Why would it?"

"If people find out Forrest left me money... that could look like a motive."

He tilted his head. "Maybe. But, you didn't know until today. Mr. Freeman can back that up."

After Troy left, I headed to the morgue and left Roberta in charge of the shop. Jessa was out sick, but the shop was slow enough that one person could handle it for a little while. I needed to stash this letter somewhere Troy would never find it.

Grandpa was behind the counter when I walked in, and Murphy bounced around at his feet. The second he saw me, he darted over, his cinnamon roll tail wagging like crazy.

"You're early," Grandpa said.

I scooped Murphy into my arms. "I just need to put something in my room."

Upstairs, I set Murphy down and pulled the envelope from under my arm. "What do I do, Murph? Hide it or destroy it?" He cocked his head. "Yeah, you're right. Probably shouldn't destroy it. Knowing my luck, it'll end up being evidence or something. Honestly, I'm surprised Troy didn't take it."

Murphy grabbed a towel from my laundry basket and ran in circles with it.

I sat on the bed, unfolded the letter, and finally read the part I'd skipped earlier.

No one could ever compare to Troy. You both watch each other and never do anything about it, so I hoped I had a chance.

I glanced at Murphy. "Forrest was out of his mind. Troy never watched me. That's just—" I paused. "Right?" Murphy flopped over, towel still in his mouth.

I stared at the letter again. The idea that someone else had noticed me watching Troy was mortifying. But worse... what if Forrest wasn't the only one who had?

I shoved the letter into the bottom of my sock drawer. "I bet it was a lucky guess on Forrest's part. Chase never said anything, and he would've teased me mercilessly if he thought I had a crush on Troy."

Murphy sneezed.

"What did I even do before I had you to talk to?" I bent down and rubbed his head. "You're very therapeutic. Thanks for listening."

He sneezed again, and I laughed. "Let's get you back to Grandpa. I think he needs you more than I do some days."

When I got back to my shop, Vivian was there. I felt nervous around her now that I knew she knew about Forrest leaving me money. She was talking to Roberta, and they both turned when I entered.

Vivian smiled. "Hello, Neeley. I was just talking to Mr. Freeman. He said he told you about the will."

"He did."

"He didn't mention your reaction. He's a little tight-lipped, so I was curious what you thought about the whole thing."

"I was shocked," I said honestly. "I told him I'm not accepting the money."

She tilted her head. "Is there a reason?"

"We weren't close. I'd feel weird taking money from someone who wasn't really even a friend."

"He always talked like you were."

I shrugged. "I'm not sure why."

"You were his first big crush."

I fought the urge to gag. But Vivian must've found something decent in Forrest—she'd married him, after all. "That was news to me."

Vivian laughed. "Forrest was always a little hard to read. I never would've ended up with him if I hadn't done all the chasing. He had a book of poetry with several poems dedicated to you. I can show them to you sometime if you want."

Roberta moved some things around, pretending not to listen. I couldn't think of a reason to want to read them.

"Isn't that awkward for you?" I asked.

Vivian's eyes narrowed, and she looked confused. "Why? Because he liked you? Forrest and I were open about past relationships and feelings. We had something special, so I didn't feel threatened by the past."

I nodded. "That's amazing, I'm not sure I could be like that."

"You just need to be secure in yourself and your relationship."

Even if I were in a secure relationship, I wouldn't want to know about someone's past girlfriends or crushes, and I would be really annoyed if my partner left money to one of those people.

She patted my arm. "You can take the money. I don't mind. You were an important part of his past, and I respect that."

"I'm not taking the money."

"Alright. Whatever you want."

Roberta handed her a vase of roses, and Vivian paid and left.

"Most people are a mystery," I said.

Roberta snickered. "That's for sure. Can you imagine leaving an old flame money in your will? If I had a husband who did that, I would dig him up and kill him again."

I laughed. "It's so weird. I didn't even know Forrest liked me. I'm really annoyed he copied off me in tests, though. He wouldn't like me if I'd known when he was alive, because I would have had something to say about that."

"It's weird he would still leave you something in a will from only three years ago. If I were Vivian, I'd be fuming." Roberta had obviously been eavesdropping when I'd read the letter out loud.

"Will you keep that quiet? It'll just give people more to talk about, and I'm not up for it."

"Of course. But for what it's worth, I think you should keep the money."

"No. I don't need it, and I feel like it should stay in his family."

"I think you should ask to see those poems."

"Gross. I don't want to see any of them."

"Who was the guy Forrest couldn't compare to?"

I shook my head. "Just someone I knew in high school."

"Was he right? Was there really someone no one else could compare to for you?"

"Yes," I admitted. "And I'm annoyed Forrest figured it out. I never told anyone."

"You must've been obvious."

"Maybe. But no one else ever said anything."

"Well, you better hope Vivian doesn't go blabbing about the money. People will start assuming you killed him for it."

"I know. There are too many things pointing at me for my liking."

"The sheriff doesn't seem concerned."

"No. He knows me better than almost anyone. Besides, he still thinks Jackie did it."

"Do you?"

"I'm not sure." I didn't want to tell her there was a lot pointing at Pedro as well. She didn't want to hear that.

Chapter 16

I sat at the diner waiting for my food to come. I came here by myself occasionally so I can stare out the window and think.

"Neeley!" Jackie said, rushing to my table and sitting across from me. "I was hoping I would run into you."

"Oh?"

She twisted a silver bracelet. "We are the two people in town everyone is talking about. How are you dealing with it?"

"I'm trying to ignore it. How are you doing?" I tried to stop myself from tapping my fingers on the table.

"Fine, now that I'm not locked up. I just hope the sheriff finds out who tried to frame me."

"You have no ideas?"

"About who framed me? No. I keep thinking maybe one of the cooks could be involved because they have access to the kitchen. I get that I look guilty, but I'm sure it will all get fixed."

"How is the diner doing?"

"It's been fine. I have a good staff. They kept things going when I was gone."

"That's good."

"Something in the back of my head keeps telling me someone should check out Pedro. He was against Forrest's winery, and he would lose a lot of money if it had been built."

"I'm sure the sheriff is looking into everyone."

"Pedro talked to me a few weeks before Forrest died. He wanted me to help him start a petition. He said we needed to stop Forrest one way or another."

"Hmm. Did you tell the sheriff?"

"No. I figured he wouldn't listen to me since he thinks I did it. He let me go, but I can tell he still thinks it was me. He might listen if you told him."

So that was it. She wanted to talk to me so I would fix things for her.

She pulled on her ponytail. "Has the sheriff taken you in for questioning?"

"No."

She frowned. "That doesn't seem fair. There's as much stuff pointing at you as me. Maybe even more. I mean,

Forrest named you in his will? That's huge. And the flowers around your shop. That looks bad."

"Are you saying you think it's me?" I asked.

"No, I just don't see why I'm the one who everyone thinks is more likely guilty."

"How did you know about the will?"

"Vivian was talking about it."

That was just lovely.

"I mean, Vivian said you were Forrest's muse. She said he was super obsessed with you before she came along, and maybe even still."

"People keep saying that, but it doesn't make sense. I hardly knew him."

Jackie's eyes narrowed. "I think the sheriff should look into you, just to be fair. He's being blinded by your friendship, and that's unprofessional."

I was glad Jackie didn't know I was the one who found the canister in her diner. That would make me look even more guilty in her eyes.

"He's not ignoring things. He looked around my shop."

"Hmm."

A server brought me my plate of fries.

"Interesting choice," she said, looking at my food. "I need to go. Enjoy." She stood and went to the kitchen.

I sighed and dumped a pile of ketchup on my plate.

Troy sat across from me, scaring me from my thoughts. "Hey." He looked at my plate. "I didn't know there was an option for a plate full of fries."

I gave him half a grin. "You have to ask for it. They give you a weird look, but only the first three or four times you do it."

"There're always a few strange people who frequent places. Does that make you one of them?"

I laughed softly. "Probably. You should have seen the looks I got when I put ketchup on my hotdog. Apparently, adults don't do things like that."

"Mustard. Everyone knows you use mustard."

"Mustard tastes like... mustard. It's not my thing." I picked up a couple of fries.

"Have you seen Jackie?"

I looked around to see if anyone was near enough to listen, leaned forward, and spoke softly. "She thinks it's unfair you aren't looking into me. I think you might need to. She said there's more stuff pointing at me than her."

He sighed. "She might have a point. I know you didn't do it, but if you were anyone else, you would be toward the top of the list."

"Then do what you would do with anyone else. I'm fine with it."

"That's more work, but I guess that's fair. I can't look like I'm favoring some people over others. I have something else you probably don't want to hear. About Forrest's obsession with you."

I groaned. "What?"

"Vivian showed me his poems. And he also has a book with pictures of you."

I grimaced. "Pictures? That's creepy."

"Most are from high school, like from the school play."

"Most?"

"Yeah, there are a few from town events."

"I'm officially creeped out." I pushed the plate away from me, appetite ruined.

"It is weird. And even weirder that Vivian seems totally fine with it." He gave me a lopsided grin. "The poems were actually decent. Vivian said you can read them."

I grabbed my straw wrapper and whipped it at him. "I don't understand why he was even interested in me. We were barely classroom acquaintances. I never said more than a few sentences to him."

Troy leaned back, clearly enjoying this far too much. "He wrote an entire poem about your lips."

I slapped both hands over my face and slid down my chair. "Oh my gosh. That is so uncomfortable."

He laughed. "It was pretty accurate, though."

I peeked through my fingers to glare at him. "You didn't read it, did you?"

He raised his brows. "Maybe."

I dropped my hands and sat back up. "I knew it. That's a violation of something."

He shrugged. "Poetic curiosity."

"Seriously, though. If anyone else read those—"

"Don't worry. I'm the only one who saw them."

"That doesn't make me feel better. That guy was mad."

Troy smiled again, softer this time. "Or maybe he just had really good taste."

My stomach fluttered. "Vivian is pretty and confident. I'm surprised she put up with that."

"She had a man over at her house when I went by. She introduced him as her boyfriend."

My mouth turned down. "Forrest isn't even buried."

"I don't think he's a new boyfriend. I think Forrest and Vivian had an interesting relationship."

"Oh. I'm so glad I didn't know anything about all this until he was dead. I might have moved."

Troy let out a soft laugh and took one of my fries. "Try not to think about it. I only told you because I figure you'll find out eventually. I'm not sure how so many rumors get around in this town. Things I don't tell anyone somehow get out."

"Hey, Sheriff," Pedro said, walking over to the table. "I saw Jackie. You let her out?"

"There are some things I need to look into."

"Hmm. I hope she isn't a danger to anyone."

"I'm not worried about that."

"I hope you're right. It would be unfortunate if she were to hurt anyone else." He nodded and walked out the front door.

"That was weird," I said, watching the door swing shut.

Troy stood and glanced out the window. "He's almost as high on my list as Jackie. There's a lot pointing at him."

"As much as me?"

He snagged another fry. "Yeah—don't worry, I'll check you out."

A guilty smirk played across his lips. He knew what he'd said, and he wasn't sorry. We were falling back into our old friendship banter, and I wasn't sure my heart could take it this time.

"Are you going to pay for those fries?" I asked as he reached for another.

He grinned. "Probably not. I'll stay at the mortuary tonight and take another look around."

"Have you been through Pedro's house?"

"I've been inside, but I haven't searched it. I don't have a good enough cause for a warrant."

"Roberta is sure he's innocent, but that could be her crush talking. He would benefit if Jackie went out of business. If he killed Forrest and blamed Jackie, that would benefit him in two ways. He would have the corner on selling alcohol."

"True." He took a fry and pointed it at me this time. "Don't go into his house."

I gave him my sweetest smile. "Why would I do that?"

"Why did you go into his store? And into the diner? I wouldn't put it past you. Besides, I have something better for you to do."

"Oh?"

His smile turned sly. "While I search your room and shop, you can change the oil in my truck. It's a trade."

I tossed a fry at him, and he caught it off his shirt and popped it into his mouth.

"How is that a trade? You search my stuff to see if I'm a criminal, and I do your maintenance?"

"I'll throw in a maple donut."

He knew me too well. I'd do just about anything for a maple donut.

"Fine," I said. The truth? I kind of liked changing oil. It made me feel capable. I'd never done it on a truck before, though. I might have to watch a few videos.

꧁❀꧂

I stared up at the undercarriage of Troy's truck. Suddenly, someone grabbed my ankle. I barely held in a scream as the creeper I was lying on rolled out from under the truck.

Troy looked down at me.

"What are you doing?" I snapped. "You could've made me mess something up or get hurt!"

"Sorry. I know nothing about vehicles."

"Then maybe don't yank people out from under them. Did you need something?"

"I finished searching your house. Murphy followed me around."

"Did you see my grandpa?"

"No. I didn't check the mortuary areas since I already searched those the other day."

I smiled. "Did you find anything incriminating?"

"No," he said, smirking, "but I did discover something strange."

I tilted my head. "What?"

"You are ridiculously neat, and you sort your socks by color."

My eyes narrowed. "You searched my drawers?"

"I searched everything," he said, entirely unapologetic. "I had to do as thorough a job as I would anywhere else. Now no one can say I'm not looking into all possibilities."

I thought of the letter from Forrest.

"Don't worry, I didn't read Forrest's letter," he said as if he'd read my mind. "Your secret crush is still a secret."

"But you went through all my stuff?" I groaned. "I'm going to have to block that out of my brain."

He gave me a grin that was pure mischief. "I found your journal. I didn't read it. Thought about it. I think I should get points for restraint."

"I don't even hide it," I muttered. "I'm confident my grandpa isn't going to read it. It's not even interesting."

"Can I have the keys to the flower shop?"

"Sure." I pulled them from my pocket and tossed them to him.

"Thanks. When I'm done, I'll go find Billie and tell her I searched it all and didn't find anything. She'll spread that around town fast enough."

"Probably."

"Are you almost done here?"

"Twenty more minutes."

"It looks like you got half the oil on your face."

I forced myself not to touch my cheek. My hands were a mess, and I'd had a small spill that was going to take some serious scrubbing. "I've never worked on a truck before. I've had a few issues."

He chuckled. "I'll be back after I look through the shop."

I nodded and rolled back under the truck. When Troy said he'd search my place the same way he would for anyone else, I hadn't taken him literally. I figured he'd do a surface-level check and call it good. I never expected him to go through my drawers.

While I worked, I kept thinking about what he might've found strange in my room. Nothing too bad came to mind, so I started to relax. My room's almost as boring as my journal, which I purposely keep dull. The last thing I wanted was someone knowing my innermost feelings.

By the time I finished with the oil, I was convinced Troy owed me two maple donuts and a chocolate milk. That had taken way longer than I planned. I wouldn't put it past him to have done it on purpose to keep me too busy to go snooping around Pedro's place.

Chapter 17

Roberta fell through the window into Pedro's front room. "Ouch." She rolled over and sat up. "How is it I keep ending up doing these things with you? Jessa's in better shape."

"Jessa doesn't believe in..." I wanted to say breaking the law, but I also wanted to pretend that wasn't what we were doing. "Well, she doesn't want to get in trouble."

"Don't get me wrong, I love the thrill of whatever it is we keep doing, but boy, do I need to get in better shape." She stretched out her back to embellish her point and palmed a sore spot that she'd landed on.

I offered my hands and helped her to her feet. We didn't have to be quiet. We'd just seen Pedro at the store, and he looked busy. He wouldn't be home anytime soon.

"What are we looking for?"

"Anything unusual. Maybe a bright purple shirt. Or at least a purple shirt with bright purple buttons."

"He sure likes that shirt."

"I'd never noticed."

"Really? Jessa teases him about it since it's so bright."

"Should we split up?"

"Okay, but only because it isn't dark. You go upstairs."

"Got it." I rushed up the stairs and went into the first room I came to. It was a small bedroom, and it wasn't any cleaner than Pedro's office had been. The bed wasn't made, and there was a mountain of laundry in the corner. I figured that was the best place to start if I wanted to find the shirt.

I didn't waste time trying to be careful. There was no easy way I could make the room more of a disaster than it already was. I grabbed laundry and tossed it to the side. Once I'd moved the entire pile to a different spot, I went through it again, putting it back where I'd gotten it. Nothing purple had stood out to me.

"Neeley!" Roberta called, clomping up the stairs. "Where are you?"

"In here!"

She came in and held up the purple shirt. "Found it."

"Where?"

"On a kitchen chair. Pedro is a mess. And guess what? It's missing a button."

I nodded. "That's what we're looking for. Let's take a picture of the missing button, put it back, and get out of here."

"We aren't looking for anything else?"

"I suppose we could."

"That's a huge pile of laundry."

I nodded. "I'm surprised he wears the purple shirt so often. He has more than twice as many clothes as me, right here." I gestured to the mess surrounding me. "I didn't look in the closet, but it's probably full as well."

Roberta sighed. "He definitely needs a wife."

I laughed. "How would that help?"

"She could nag him to put away his clothes, if nothing else."

"Is that what you want marriage to be? Constantly nagging?"

"No, but sometimes I think I need someone to nag me. My house isn't this messy, but I could use a maid. I put my clothes away. I don't fold them, but I shove them in a drawer."

That explained all Roberta's wrinkled clothing.

She pulled open the closet doors and peeked in. "At least he hangs things up."

A door slamming downstairs made us pause.

"How does this keep happening?" I whispered.

Roberta tossed the shirt she was holding onto the pile of clothes. "What do we do?"

I looked around, unsure. There was a window, but I couldn't imagine Roberta getting out from the second floor.

"We might have to hide."

"What if he's staying for the day?" Her eyes were wide. "You get out. I've got this."

I shook my head. "This isn't the same as at the store. You can't say you were arranging his milk."

"Folding his clothes?"

I rolled my eyes. "Because that's not creepy?"

Whistling and footsteps on the stairs had me in a panic.

"Just get out!" Roberta said, rushing into the hall. I slapped myself on the forehead. This was a disaster.

Pedro yelped. "Roberta! What are you doing here? Don't tell me you came to check for expired food."

I went to the window and pulled it open. The ground wasn't terribly far, if I could lower myself.

"Do you want the truth, Pedro?" Roberta was saying.

"The truth would be nice. Do I need to call the police?"

I cringed. I couldn't leave Roberta to deal with that alone.

"I'm sorry!" Roberta said. "I know this looks like I'm a crazy stalker or something, but well... maybe I am."

"You? A stalker?"

Roberta let out a long, exaggerated sigh. "I like you, Pedro. I've liked you for years."

Silence.

My heart was pounding from almost being caught, and even harder for whatever emotional turmoil Roberta must be going through.

"You like me?" he finally said.

"Yes."

"Why didn't you tell me?"

"It's awkward."

"Come downstairs, let's talk."

I put my left leg over the window and pulled myself out. I scraped my arm as I tried to lower myself, but I could worry about that later. I wasn't going to be able to close the window behind me. Pedro would assume Roberta had opened it and probably be more weirded out than he already was.

I held onto the windowsill and put my knees against the side of the house. The windowsill dug into my hands, and I cringed as I let my legs go straight. It was only a four-foot drop from my dangling feet to the grass, but it felt higher. I was going to have to drop. My hands stung, and my arms were burning.

Someone wrapped their arms around my legs, and I held in a yell.

"Let go, Neeley," Troy said.

I let go and slid down into Troy's arms.

"Wow, do I have good intuition," he said.

I stepped away and rubbed my hands. "Or good luck."

He laughed. "There was no luck involved. I've walked by several times today to make sure you weren't here. Come on. Let's get out of here. I saw Pedro go inside, which I assume is why you went out that way."

I followed him out to his truck, and he opened the passenger side. I climbed in and examined my arm. It was scraped, but not bleeding.

Troy got in and drove down the road. "You know I could arrest you for breaking and entering?"

I glanced at him and smiled. "You mean exiting? And I didn't break anything."

"I thought Roberta or Jessa would be with you."

"Roberta's still in there."

He braked, and I put my hand on the dashboard.

"And you're leaving her?" he demanded.

"She did that on her own. As soon as Pedro came in, she went out and told him she was his stalker and that she liked him. I'm not sure what happened after that."

He whistled. "Wow. You owe her."

"I know, but I'm pretty sure she does like him. Maybe I did her a favor... depending on what he says. And it might be lame if he likes her and then goes to jail."

"Did you find anything?"

"We found a bright purple shirt with a missing button."

"So he was at the mortuary."

"It appears that way."

He tapped the steering wheel as he drove off. I guess I was going home. It was good I hadn't driven.

"I don't get this," he said. "There's about an equal amount of evidence pointing at Pedro, Jackie, and you. I was positive it was Jackie, and now I'm not sure."

"Jackie could have been framed by Pedro. All he would have had to do was put that canister in her diner."

"What about her lying about not caring about the winery?"

I rubbed my hand and thought. "Maybe she didn't want to look like an angry competitor?"

He moved his jaw as he thought. "You're leaning toward Pedro?"

"Kind of, but I hope it isn't him. Especially if he likes Roberta. Do you still think it's Jackie?"

"I don't know. The button tells me Pedro broke into the mortuary. We also know he broke into Vivian's house, but then, so did you."

"I had a good reason."

"In his mind, he might have as well. Even if he broke in, we don't know why. He might not be the killer."

"That seems unlikely. What reason could he have?"

"Think about another person's perspective on you. You keep breaking into places. If they didn't know what you were doing, it would look bad, and it is illegal. I could arrest you right now, no one would bat an eye."

"But you won't."

"But I could. And I might if you keep doing it. Then I would know you weren't getting into trouble."

I looked out the window and tried to think of a comeback, but I didn't have anything. He was right. If someone snooped through my house, I would be mad. I was still annoyed that Troy had gone through my things, and I'd told him he could.

"Are you coming to book club?" I finally asked, just to have something to say.

"Maybe. If nothing weird happens."

"Weird like what?"

"Who knows? Things have been crazy lately. I swear crime in the county has risen a huge amount in the last year."

"We aren't a huge county."

"No, but we're having our issues."

"What's the craziest thing going on right now?"

"Besides Forrest's murder? Hmm. Probably Diego Torres."

The name sounded familiar, but I couldn't place it. "Who?"

"He's a possible drug dealer who has gone missing. Like, not your everyday street drug dealer. Like, big house, nice cars, no one can touch him kind of dealer."

"Are you trying to find him?"

"Not yet. He hasn't been reported missing. It's only rumors. I'm not sure we have the resources to mess with that group."

"If you need someone to sneak into his house, I'm your girl."

He laughed as he pulled up to the morgue. "I probably shouldn't have told you about it. Stay away from all that stuff. You better believe his house is full of cameras."

"Does he live in Crystal Rock?"

"No. A smaller town."

"I didn't know we had stuff like that happening."

"There are a few groups I have my eye on. I don't have the manpower to take them down, and no other cities are offering to help."

He parked, and I climbed out. I wouldn't think about drug dealers. I had enough to keep myself occupied. Still, I wasn't sure I wanted Troy dealing with that either. Why had he become a sheriff? It was a dangerous job.

Troy came over and crossed his arms. "I want you to promise you won't break into anyone else's house."

I crossed my arms and mimicked him. "For how long?"

"Forever."

"Hmm, I'm going to say no. Who knows when I might *need* to?"

"Fine, but next time I catch you, I'm taking you in."

I smiled. "Fine. Next time, you won't catch me."

"You know it's dangerous? I literally caught you this time. You could have broken something."

"But I didn't."

"Because I caught you."

"It wasn't that high."

"I swear, between you and Harmony, I'm never going to rest."

My smile faded. "I don't like sharing. Harmony should get her own person to bother."

He laughed. "Does that make me your person?"

"I like to think so." I smiled to show I was joking, but I wasn't. I didn't know Chase's wife, but from the way Troy talked, he spent a lot of time with her.

"Don't worry. You're my priority."

I was sure amusement flickered in my eyes. "I hope so. If I do break into any places, yours is next on my list. Just to make us even."

"You told me I could."

"I didn't think you would be so thorough."

"Just be thankful you didn't have anything embarrassing."

I nodded. "I better go in. Refreshments are mine tonight. I need to make something for book club."

I went inside and to the kitchen. Flirting with Troy was too much fun while it was happening, and unbearable when it ended. I needed to stop before it killed me.

Chapter 18

"What do you want from me, man?" Troy said, looking down at Murphy. Murphy had gotten Troy to pick him up, and he was lying on his back, staring up at him expectantly.

Patty laughed. "He wants you to rub his stomach. Can't you tell?"

Troy rubbed Murphy's stomach, and the pug closed his eyes, enjoying it.

"I bet Murphy liked this book," Lydia said. "The dog saved the day—twice."

"When I read books with animals, I always think I might get one, but the care is too much for me," Billie said. "I can't handle anything that needs attention."

Everyone laughed when Murphy began making a weird nasally sound with his nose. I never knew pugs could make so many odd noises until I got him.

"I think we might be reading too many books a month," Jim said. "I'm struggling to keep up."

"You think one book a week is too much?" Patty asked. "They're all fairly short."

"I guess I'm not as big of a reader as the rest of you."

"You don't have to come every week," Billie said.

Jim chuckled. "I don't want to miss out on anything weird that might happen. Besides, I get most of my gossip here. Does anyone have anything to share?"

"Forrest Cutler wrote a bunch of poems about Neeley," Lydia said. "That's gossip worthy."

I groaned. "Come on, you guys. I'm trying not to think about that. And who told?" I looked at Roberta.

She held up her hands. "It wasn't me."

"What kind of poems?" Jim asked, ignoring my discomfort.

"I don't know," Lydia said, "but I'm assuming whatever they are, they aren't the kind of thing a married guy should have been writing."

"We don't know when he wrote them," I protested. "They could be old."

Roberta peeked over at Troy. "I bet the sheriff read them."

He shrugged. "I had to."

"And? Were they romantic?"

"Yep."

"Tell us about them."

"Yeah, did you memorize any of them?" Patty asked.

I rolled my eyes. "Why would he memorize them? Can we get back to the book?" I knew I sounded desperate but didn't care.

Troy stopped rubbing Murphy's stomach, and the dog growled under his breath and batted at Troy's hand.

I grinned. "That means you aren't allowed to stop."

Troy started up again. "Bossy dog."

"Poor Sheriff McGregor. He never gets to do anything fun," Patty teased. "There's always someone bossing him around."

He smiled. "It's alright. What else do I have to do?"

"The sheriff needs a wife!" Roberta said. "I keep saying it. No one should work all the time."

Jessa shook her head. "Leave the boy alone."

"My niece is nice," Roberta said.

"I have a cousin he could date," Patty added.

Troy smirked. "You're all crazy."

"Just let us do this service for you," Roberta said. "We would all love to see you happily settled."

"How about we do that service for you first?" he asked.

Roberta smiled. "I'm doing fine on my own. I have a date with Pedro on Saturday. When's the last time you had a date?"

Troy kept rubbing Murphy's stomach and looked up at the ceiling. "I don't know. It's been a while, but that's by choice. I don't need you all throwing women at me."

"If Troy got married, he would be even busier, then he couldn't come to book club," I said.

Billie slapped the table with her hand. "We don't want that. We need all the young blood we can get here."

"Or Neeley can marry him," Jim proposed with a gleam in his eye. "Then she would keep him here."

I rolled my eyes. "You guys are so funny."

"You would be adorable together," Patty said. "Have you ever thought about dating?"

"You guys!" I said. "Let's go back to the book."

Jim laughed. "That's either a really hard yes, or a really hard no."

"Don't bug them," Jessa said. "You know both of them are broken."

Troy chuckled, and I narrowed my eyes.

"What do you mean, 'broken'?" I asked.

"You both claim you can only be in love once. That means you've lost your chance."

Lydia gave me a sly side smile. "Haven't the two of you been friends since birth?"

"Kindergarten," I corrected her.

"Maybe they were both in love with each other and didn't know it."

Billie laughed and slapped her leg. "Wouldn't that be something?"

"I love those kinds of movies," Roberta said.

Patty nodded. "I would watch it."

"Not if they never get together, though," Lydia said.

Everyone in the room was staring at us. I squirmed. I wasn't going to outright lie, but I also wasn't going to let Troy know the truth. He looked amused by the entire thing.

"Well?" Billie said. "Aren't you going to say something?"

Troy rubbed his chin. "If we had been in love, don't you think it would be really weird we went for fifteen years without talking?"

"Misunderstandings cause those types of things," Patty said.

"Oh no," I said, standing. "I left one of the coolers open at the flower shop after I cleaned it earlier. I'll be right back."

Billie laughed. "Well, if Neeley doesn't look guilty, I don't know who does."

I hurried out of the room and ignored all the laughter. I realized I was leaving Troy to the wolves, but I couldn't handle this. If I had to hear Troy admit out loud that it hadn't been me, it would break me.

I rushed down the hill, trying not to trip in the dark. It had rained earlier, and I didn't want to slide. By the time I got back, I was sure the subject would change. I was such a coward. Instead of running away, I should have turned things around and asked Jim and Billie why they weren't dating.

I smiled. That would be a funny combination.

Since I hadn't really forgotten to shut the cooler, I walked over to the shop and pulled on the handle to make sure it was locked, then started back up the hill.

A sound to the right made me pause. There were several large trees on the hill, and it would be easy to hide behind one. It could also be an animal...

Something whizzed past my head, and I dropped to the ground. I took a deep breath and ignored the mud under my hands. A rock slammed into the ground next to me, so I jumped up and ran. I heard rocks landing behind me and felt lucky whoever was out there had a poor aim.

Footsteps sounded behind me.

I ran harder, my slick shoes trying to take me down with each step. If I hadn't been insecure, I wouldn't be out here, possibly running for my life. I spotted the lights from the morgue up ahead and ignored the twigs cracking behind me. No more rocks came flying, but I didn't turn to see who it might be.

I flew up the morgue steps and pushed through the heavy door, slamming it behind me. I leaned against the door as my chest heaved. I took several calming breaths, then headed for the wide staircase. I took the steps slowly, my legs trembling.

I should tell Troy. But what if he went out there and got hurt? I didn't want him walking straight into danger for me. It was likely the person had taken off, assuming I would call the cops. It was probably over, but perhaps... it was time to tell him, anyway.

I entered the room in the middle of a Billie and Jim fight. Those were getting too common. Everyone stopped talking and stared at me.

"What happened?" Troy asked, getting to his feet. He handed Murphy to Patty.

"What do you mean?" I looked down at the mud covering me. I'd been concentrating on getting away, not the mud. It was even covering my hands. "Oh. I fell."

Troy raised his eyebrow. "You fell? Why don't you go change?"

I nodded and left the room. Troy followed me. "What really happened?"

I cringed as I looked at my muddy footprints going along the hallway.

"Someone was out there in the dark. I didn't see them, but they threw rocks at me and chased me up the hill."

"Are you hurt?"

"No, just dirty."

"Tell everyone to stay inside until I say."

"You can't go out there alone. They could be hiding anywhere."

Troy pulled out his gun. "I'll be fine. Stay here." He turned and ran down the hall.

"You're off duty!" I shouted after him. When he didn't listen, I chased after him and grabbed him around the waist. "Get backup!"

He tried to turn, but I held on tight. "There's no time—and no one to call."

"You might get killed."

"I won't. Go back." He grabbed me and pulled me awkwardly around.

I still had him in an iron grip. "No."

I felt something brush my head that I would pretend was a kiss.

He pulled back just enough to look at me. "Just let me check," he said, voice low.

I hesitated, then nodded and stepped away. My arms felt cold—and stiff—without him in them. Reluctantly, I turned and walked back into the room.

"Troy said everyone needs to stay here."

"Why?" Billie asked.

"There's someone outside, hiding."

"That means you're onto something, right?" Roberta asked. "I bet it's Jackie."

"I'm not sure what it means. You all keep talking, I'll change."

I took a thirty-second shower once in my room and pulled on clean clothes, then went back to my guests. They had pulled back the curtains and turned off the lights. They were all squished together, watching out the window.

"Did you see anything?" I asked.

"It's too dark," Roberta said. "You should get lights put all around this place."

"And probably lock the front doors. Do you ever do that?" Jim asked.

"Only after nine. Grandpa doesn't want the doors locked when people might come. Not that many do. People call to arrange things over coming here most of the time."

I went on my toes and tried to peer out into the darkness, but it was impossible to see anything.

"What are you all looking at?" Troy asked, flipping on the light.

Roberta squealed and turned around, and the rest of us jumped.

"Did you see anything?" Jim asked.

"No. There were some footprints in the mud, but it's going to be impossible to get a good look at them until tomorrow. And that's if it doesn't rain. The prints are mixed in with Neeley's, so it might be hard. I took a bad picture that might identify the type of shoe. It was about the same size as Neeley's."

"That means it wasn't Pedro," Roberta declared. "He has huge shoes."

I nodded. "Whoever it was had a bad aim and wasn't fast. They didn't catch up to me and fell behind quickly."

"I don't want anyone leaving without me going out with them to their car or being escorted off the grounds safely," Troy said. "Understand?"

Everyone nodded.

"This is getting out of control," Billie said. "You need to solve this and arrest someone."

Jim twisted his cane in his hands. "You're the one who always tells us you know how to solve all the mysteries by the end of the first chapter. Why don't you solve it?"

Billie's eyes narrowed. "I have a guess, and I'm probably right, but I don't have any evidence, so anything I say would only be my opinion. That's not enough to arrest someone on."

"I doubt the sheriff would arrest someone because you guessed something, anyway."

"No one needs to solve anything," Troy said. "I'll figure it out."

"Tomorrow is Forrest's funeral," Jessa said. "Is anyone going to go?"

"I will," Patty said. "I do feel bad for Vivian."

Billie nodded. "And everyone in town will be there. Everyone is curious."

I was undecided. With all the stuff I'd found out this last while, I wasn't sure it was a place I should be. People were already gossiping about me regarding Forrest. Going to the funeral might make it worse.

Some mortuaries have the funeral in their building, but we didn't have a room nice enough. Most people rented a building in Crystal Rock, but some did it outside in the grass near the cemetery. I'd kept telling Grandpa we should make a nice big area, but he didn't want to put in the time. This place was huge; it wouldn't be hard to add something.

"Where is the funeral?" Roberta asked.

"The cemetery," I said.

"Oh good. I like it better when people don't go out of town for it. Are you going, Neeley?"

I shrugged. "Probably not."

Chapter 19

"I forgot to check on the food!" Vivian said, pulling me to the side. Chairs lined the grass near the cemetery, and guests trickled in. I'd been here to help set up, but I had been ready to leave when she grabbed me.

"The food?" I asked.

"Yes! Jackie is catering, but I haven't talked to her all day. She isn't answering her phone. Will you go to the diner and see what's happening?"

I gave her a fake smile. "No problem." I would rather check the food than stay here. I hurried around the hill to my red Mazda and jumped inside. When I got to the diner, there were no cars there. Jackie must have closed for the funeral. I parked and went to the front doors. A sign said what I expected.

I walked around the back and knocked. When no one answered, I opened the back door.

"Jackie?" I called. The lights were off, and no one answered. "Jackie!" I yelled louder. I looked down at the muddy boots by the door and frowned. Placing my foot next to them, I noticed they were about the same size as my foot.

"Hmm. What have we been up to, Jackie?" Anyone could walk around in the mud. It didn't mean anything. I pulled out my phone and texted Troy, asking him to send me a picture of the print he took last night. A minute later, it came.

The photo was dark and so was the footprint, but it had a distinct wavy pattern. I turned the boot over and sucked in a breath. The boot had the same pattern. I took a picture and sent it to Troy. I frowned at the gold glitter surrounding them.

The long counter tops in the diner were lined with rolls, salads, and small sandwiches. This must be what Vivian was looking for. But where was Jackie?

A small thump sounded from above me.

I grabbed a flour-covered rolling pin from the counter and went through a short hallway and over to a narrow staircase. I'd only been over here once and it was years ago. Upstairs was a small room that Jackie used to hold supplies—or at least she had at one point.

My foot touched the first metal step and made a small creak. I kept a tight grip on the rolling pin as I went up the steps as softly as possible. At the top of the stairs was a small wooden door with dings all over it.

I took a breath before I pushed the door open.

Jackie spun around and glared at me. "What are you doing here?"

I lowered the rolling pin. "Vivian sent me. She said she'd been texting you about the food and you weren't answering."

"The food? That's not until tomorrow."

"No, it's today. It looks like you have it all ready down there."

Jackie blinked and rubbed her eyes. "I came up here to get something, and I got so sleepy. I might have fallen asleep and gotten confused." She appeared disheveled.

"You don't know if you were asleep?"

"I was up late last night getting ready. I'm tired."

"You better call Vivian. She's freaking out."

I looked around the small room. It had shelves on all four walls, and they were full of ingredients. In one corner was a small humidifier. It was making a small hum, but no steam was coming out.

I pointed at it. "You need humidity up here?"

"What?" She frowned and pushed past me. "I need to grab some headache meds and get things ready."

I followed her down the steps. "Are they eating here?"

"Yes. Right after the funeral. I can't believe I'm so disorganized. A bad night shouldn't make me this off."

I wondered if it was a night of preparing, or a night of chasing people through the mud.

"Let me help you," I said when we got into the kitchen. "What can I do?"

"Umm... the rolls and salad should be on all the tables. I should have some servers coming any minute."

I grabbed a bowl of rolls and a salad and took them out to a table. Lace tablecloths hung over all the tables, and a vase with one rose sat in the middle of each one. I put down the rolls and salad and went back to the kitchen.

"It looks like someone was out in the mud last night," I said, pointing at the boots.

Jackie looked over and frowned. "I wonder who left those there. I don't need mud in the kitchen." She picked up the boots and tossed them in the garbage.

A man came in and began washing his hands. I recognized him as one of the servers.

"Kale, will you take that garbage out?"

"Sure," he said, taking the half-full bag.

"It could still hold a lot more," I said.

Jackie ignored me.

"I'm going to go back to the funeral," I said, letting myself out the back. I rushed to my car and got there in record time. I needed to find Troy.

The funeral had begun, and Troy was sitting in the back row. I sat next to him. "Did you get the picture?" I whispered.

"No. I silenced my phone." He pulled it out and looked at it. "Where was this?"

"The diner. Jackie's acting weird. She said she was asleep in her storage room, and she was confused. I bet she was out all night throwing rocks at people."

"Hmm."

We went quiet as a man spoke. When he was finished, Vivian stood. I wanted to leave, but it would seem rude to get up in the middle of a funeral.

"Forrest Cutler was a great man," Vivian began. "He had a wonderful enthusiasm for life. He loved so many things, and had so many ideas. Forrest loved art and music. He was passionate about his ideas."

I blocked her voice out at that point and looked around at the people listening to her. Most of them I knew. I spotted everyone from the book club—and Pedro. He was sitting by Roberta. I smiled. I hoped something worked out for them. If he wasn't the killer, anyway.

A girl about ten who was sitting in front of us turned to the woman next to her and held up a gold purse.

"I don't want to hold Aunt Viv's purse. It gets glitter on everything," the girl complained.

"Shh," the woman said. "Just put it on your lap and be careful. She takes that thing everywhere and will be mad if you ruin it."

"But it's getting all over my dress!"

I covered my mouth with one hand and looked at Troy. He was listening to Vivian. Somehow, we'd gotten it wrong. Completely wrong, and it should have been so obvious.

"What is it?" Troy asked, leaning near me.

"It was Vivian. It's always the jealous, greedy wife. Why didn't we see it? It's like, textbook obvious."

Troy's brows came together, and I stood up.

"Sit," he whispered loudly.

I shook my head. My eyes locked with Vivian's, and she smiled.

She gestured to me. "Back there, we have another thing that Forrest loved to a ridiculous degree."

Everyone turned and looked at me.

"Neeley was the inspiration for a lot of Forrest's poetry. I love that she inspired him."

"No, you don't," I said. "You hate it."

She laughed. "No, everyone who knows Forrest and me know we have a strange marriage. I can admire someone Forrest takes an interest in."

"Then why did you try to frame me for his murder?"

It occurred to me as soon as I said it that more than one

person in the world had glittery things. It didn't matter. I was too far in.

"What are you talking about?" she asked. I had everyone's attention.

"I think the reason you failed is because you tried to frame not one, not two, but three people. You overdid it, Vivian."

Vivian rubbed her lips together and twisted her wedding ring. "Are you saying I killed Forrest?"

"I am." I looked down at Troy. He had sunk down into his chair. He thought I was wrong, and possibly crazy.

"Why would I kill Forrest?"

"He was about to use all your money to buy a business that was doomed to fail. You are financially comfortable, but you would be ruined if that happened. You needed someone to blame, so why not blame the woman your husband was oddly obsessed with?"

"This is ridiculous."

I shrugged. "I agree. And for all the gossips in the town, there was never anything going on with Forrest and me. I never even liked him as a friend."

Vivian scowled. "That's not true! You dated in high school. I've seen the pictures! And I don't care. I have a boyfriend on the side, so why would it bother me? We never hid that stuff from each other."

"We went on one date." How many times was I going to have to say this? "You planned this in advance. So far in advance, that you are the only one who could have done it. Forrest told you his plans before he told anyone else. You had time to plant the datura in with my moonflowers to frame me."

"Sheriff? You can't let her slander me like this!" Vivian said, marching down a row between the chairs. She stopped ten feet from me.

Troy held up his hands.

"Of course you aren't any help!" She scowled violently.

"And that's why you switched who you were trying to frame," I said, "but let's get to that later. You made something for Forrest to drink at the town meeting. You crushed up datura and put it in. You made sure the two of you got to the table first, so he would drink it the fastest. You tasted yours next and said there was something wrong with the drink."

Roberta stood and pointed to her. "And then you dropped the entire bowl so no one else could taste it and disagree! That made it look like it was Neeley's fault! And you dropped a moonflower in the other bowl at the end of the night to point suspicion that way!"

I nodded. "Exactly."

"That's crazy," she said. "I loved Forrest."

"You realized you set up the wrong person, because the sheriff has been my best friend for years, and he knows I would never do it. Next, you went after Jackie, placing the datura leaves in her diner. You knew she secretly didn't want the winery to come in, and you knew her sales figures would prove that."

She put her hands on her hips. "I can't believe you interrupted a funeral to spout off these lies!"

"You must have felt like the evidence wasn't enough, so you began doing things to point at Pedro. You even got his button somehow and snuck it into the morgue."

"What?" Pedro said. "Why haven't I heard about this?"

I ignored him. He'd also made himself look guilty by breaking into Vivian's house. "You must have still hoped that somehow it would be pinned on me, so you went to the flower shop and tore out the datura to make it look like I was hiding the evidence, and then you tossed Pedro's name tag in there. You overdid it, Vivian." I'd grown secure in my theory now. It had to be her. "By trying to frame so many people, you made it all come back to you."

"There is no evidence pointing at me, because I didn't do it!"

"There is evidence. Evidence at the morgue, and at the diner. You couldn't just stop. What did you do to Jackie?"

"I didn't touch Jackie." She threw her arms up dramatically.

"You put a humidifier in her diner, pumping out something. It made her fall asleep and get disoriented. You sent me to check on her, because you knew I would be sure to see the muddy boots you used when you were throwing rocks at me last night."

"That's insane," Vivian said. "Do you know how pathetic this sounds? I was home all night."

A man in the front row stood. "You left last night for a few hours."

"Shut up, Ted!" Vivian yelled.

Ted glared at her. "If you're lying about where you were, it makes me wonder if what this woman is saying is true."

"Of course it is," Roberta said.

I smiled. I was glad she had confidence in me.

"I might have stepped out for a few minutes," she said.

"No," Ted said. "You were gone for a long time. I'm not covering for you if you killed Forrest. You also had some muddy boots you were carrying around this morning."

"You left glitter from your purse at the mortuary and at the diner," I said.

Vivian stomped toward me, and Troy jumped up and stood in front of me. I moved around him. Vivian was at least three inches shorter than me and more concerned with her nails than doing anything to build muscle.

Troy grabbed me around the waist and pulled me back to him. "Not at a funeral," he muttered.

"What is wrong with all the men in this town?" Vivian said, gritting her teeth. "You have to have everyone's attention?"

"I don't try to get anyone's attention. I don't know what Forrest's deal was."

"Do you know how hard it is to live in the shadow of someone who appears perfect? Forrest told me when we got married that he was never going to get over you. I told him it was fine, but there is only so much obsessing I can take!"

"So, it wasn't about the winery?" Roberta asked.

"It was completely about the winery! He was trying to ruin us, and for what? A stupid dream. It might be fine if it were his only dream, but he was onto something new every year!"

Troy took a step toward her. "And you figured you might as well take Neeley down in the process?"

Her eyes narrowed. "I know you're trying to get me to confess to everything. I know my rights." She spun around and rushed in the opposite direction.

Troy caught up to her and had her cuffed in no time. He led her from the crowd, and everyone started talking at once.

An older man in the front waved his arms to get people's attention. I thought I recognized him as Forrest's dad, but it had been a while since I'd seen him. "People, people! Let's call it a wrap. The food at the diner is already paid for, we might as well meet there."

Jessa made her way over to me. "That was crazy. I can't believe you figured it all out."

"Me neither. It all came to me at once, so I'm not sure anything I said made sense. I was sure it was Pedro, but I wanted to keep that to myself for Roberta's sake."

"Are you going to the diner?"

"No. I'm going to go tell Grandpa what happened, then I'm going to take Murphy for a nice quiet walk so I can think. Or I might go to my room and take a nap. It's anyone's guess."

Jessa laughed. "Well, give me a call if you need to talk."

I nodded. "I will. Eat some rolls for me, they looked good."

"You know I'm all about rolls."

Everyone had left quickly, and I was left standing there with all the chairs. I wasn't going for a walk or to bed. I would be spending the next while folding up chairs.

Chapter 20

I woke up to Murphy licking my elbow. "What are you doing, Murph?" I rolled over and pulled my arms securely under the blanket. "Go back to sleep."

The sun shone through the cracks in the curtains, but I figured it was a good day to sleep in. Murphy crawled up near my head and squished himself between me and the headboard, and then he stuck one paw in my face.

Someone knocked, and I sighed. "Come in."

I was expecting Grandpa, but it was Troy.

He looked at me and laughed. "That looks comfy."

"He has a bed. A nice comfy, expensive bed, and somehow, we end up like this."

Troy came over and picked Murphy up. The energetic pug tried climbing up Troy and rested his front paws over his shoulder.

"Great. You take him, I'll sleep."

"Don't you want to know what happened last night?"

I sat up and pushed my hair out of my eyes. "What happened?"

"Vivian confessed to everything. She even confessed to how she did everything, right down to swiping Pedro's button. She put in a lot of effort. I think you were right. She overdid it by trying to frame too many people."

"What's next, then?"

"I'm hoping for a nice, relaxing weekend. It hasn't happened in a while."

"You don't want to look into the disappearance of that drug guy?"

"I have been a bit. I'm not sure where to start. Since no one has reported it, things get tricky. There's a good chance he's hiding because there was a lot of evidence building up against him."

"If you need me, I'm here."

He shook his head. "I'll deal with it. You sell flowers and read your mysteries."

"I'm glad we're getting you hooked on them."

"I read some when I was a kid. *The Hardy Boys,* or something like that."

"What do you read now when you get to choose?"

"Sci-fi or fantasy. Not deep fantasy. I like it light and easy. Nothing that keeps me up at night thinking. I have too much of that going on as it is."

I yawned. "Why did you get up so early? You should be tired."

"Early? It's after ten. I've been up for hours."

"It's good the shop isn't open today." I tried to smooth down my hair, knowing it most likely looked wild. "Is Jackie mad at you for locking her up?"

"She's being surprisingly nice about that. I'd be mad, but she said she gets it."

Murphy wiggled around, and Troy put him down.

"I'm feeling good," he said. "There are no cases weighing on my mind. It's been a while since that happened. Do you want to go get breakfast? I'm off today."

"At the diner?"

"I hope not. I've seen enough of that place this week. What if we drive into Crystal Rock? That gives us a few options."

"Sounds good. Can I shower first?"

"Yep. If you give me Murphy's leash, I'll go walk him around."

I went to my dresser and grabbed the leash. "You're the best." I handed it to him and tried not to react to his hand brushing mine. I watched them leave the room, unsure which one was more adorable.

Troy was lucky I'd forgotten the name of the man who'd disappeared. If I hadn't, I might be looking him up. Not that I wanted to get involved in something like that. If I didn't stop butting into things, my life might turn into a mess.

I pulled out a clean shirt and smiled to myself. No one was framing me, Murphy was getting his morning walk, and I was going to breakfast with the boy I'd been in love with since I was sixteen.

Was it a date? Probably not. Was I going to pretend it was? You better believe it.

It was shaping up to be a perfect Saturday. Unless, of course, the missing drug guy turned up in the Crystal Rock parking lot.

I slipped my notebook into my purse. Just in case.

About the Author

Kristy Dixon started writing stories at age seven and never stopped. These days, she writes cozy mysteries full of quirky characters, small-town charm, and the occasional dead body. She also writes YA novels when the teens in her head get too loud to ignore. Kristy lives with her husband, kids, one spoiled cat, and a flock of chickens who think they run the place. When she's not writing or wrangling her crew, she's likely playing board games, plotting murders (fictional, of course), or dreaming about cookies.

Also By Kristy Dixon

<u>Cozy Mystery</u>
Murder With a Side of Bacon
Murder With a Hint of Cinnamon
Murder With a Fudge Brownie to Go
Murder With a Splash of Vanilla
Murder With a Drizzle of Syrup
Murder With a Slice of Pie
Murder With a Swirl of Blueberry
Suite Lies and Alibis
Not So Suite Caroline

Made in the USA
Monee, IL
11 November 2025

34410956R00125